SHOWDOWN

"Matt!" yelled Festus. "Someone's just hit the bank!"

A .44/40 slug fired from across the street struck the office door and drove a sharp sliver of wood into Festus' right cheek. He winced and slammed shut the door, dropping to the floor where he wormed his way over to the rifle rack. A second bullet shattered one of the front windows, struck one of the cell bars and richochetted, whizzing meanly through the office.

Matt Dillon rolled from the bunk fully dressed, and snatched up a nearby Winchester. "Keep that rifleman busy!" he yelled over his shoulder as he yanked open the rear door.

A masked man came running into the alleyway. "Damn you, Dillon!" he shouted, raising his rifle. Matt saw him aim point blank and pull the trigger . . .

Be sure to read the first exciting AWARD book in the action-packed GUNSMOKE series:

AN1283   THE RENEGADES

GUNSMOKE

#2
SHOOTOUT

Jackson Flynn

Copies of this printing
distributed in the United Kingdom by
Universal-Tandem Publishing Company, Ltd.

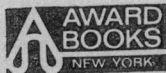

AWARD
BOOKS
NEW YORK

AWARD BOOKS are published by
Universal-Award House, Inc., a subsidiary of
Universal Publishing and Distributing Corporation,
235 East Forty-fifth Street, New York, N.Y. 10017.

Manufactured in the United States of America

Chapter 1

Trouble came to a rolling boil in Pawnee, Harker County, Kansas, one rainy Saturday night in September. You were either on the side of the Establishment, represented by Ned Grant for over twenty years in Pawnee *and* Harker County, or you were inclined to lean cautiously toward the so-called Law and Order group. This group was still in the minority but was gaining strength every month from the leading professional and businessmen of Pawnee, not to mention the clergy and the irate "decent" women of the town. Their leader was Sam Burkitt, a one-armed Union veteran of the Civil War, who had left his right arm on Little Round Top at Gettysburg.

Ned Grant had held all the aces in Pawnee and Harker County for a long time, backed by Sheriff Bert Quinn for the past ten long years or so—long, that is, for those who knew that the sheriffdom of Harker County—instead of being a duly elected office voted on by the honest citizens of the district—was really an appointive office, won through the spoils system established by Ned Grant. The sheriff of Harker County ruled his bailiwick from Pawnee, the county seat, which also had been established by Ned Grant. Sheriff Quinn was the harsh, pistol-whipping right arm of the little, unlawful empire created by the brutal Ned Grant.

Barney Grant, Ned Grant's beloved only son, said to be the progeny of Ned and a madam of one of Ned's bawdy houses in Pawnee who had disappeared shortly after Barney's birth, had been drinking for the past two days that rainy Saturday night. He had been swaggering up and down Grant Street, the main thoroughfare of Pawnee, noisily patronizing every saloon in town. There were quite a few saloons, and Ned Grant either owned some of them outright or held a fifty-one percent interest in them. In fact, the first building in Pawnee had been an old army tent over a wooden frame, stocked with rotgut liquor by none other than Ned Grant. That had been in the days when white men were either hunting buffalo or Indians along the Pawnee River.

Barney usually ended up his drinking bouts at the Bella Union, which had developed from his father's framed army tent. It had been his original business venture on the banks of the Pawnee when he had come west after service in the Confederate army. Actually he had ridden with Quantrill's guerrillas and had gotten his initial business stake from loot taken during Quantrill's bloody raid on Lawrence, Kansas. To cover up his service with Quantrill and how he had gotten the money to start his saloon business, Ned Grant had given it a name that would certainly cast no suspicions on his loyalties—the Bella Union.

Barney usually dominated the Bella Union. It was his playpen, his sandbox, so to speak, and in it he was like a dog in the manger. He was a mean, vicious, rather stupid young man of twenty years who really fancied himself quite a gunslinger. He was always safe in his cocksure attitude, for he knew as long as Sheriff Bert Quinn ruled Harker County and Pawnee—and Ned Grant ruled Bert Quinn—he could get away with damned near anything short of coldblooded murder.

That rainy September night Barney Grant came swaggering into the Bella Union and took his place at the end of the bar not far from the front door, with his back to the wall, which was his usual stance for good reason— Barney Grant always feared that shot in the dark or the knife in the back. He came into the Bella Union full of good whiskey and bad intentions. In short, there was whiskey on his breath and blood in his small, mean eyes.

The Bella Union was crowded. It was usually crowded. The bar was fully lined with hard-drinking men, both Grant men and Law and Order men; the gambling tables were doing a rousing business; the roulette wheels whirled and the chuck-a-luck cages twirled; the girls upstairs had hardly a moment's breather between customers. Business was better than good—it was payday in Pawnee.

Barney ordered whiskey and quickly downed two glasses. He was raising his glass for the third time when his eyes came into focus on a tall, bearded man standing at the bar not far him, who was drinking with his left hand. His right coat sleeve was pinned to the front of his coat. For a second or two it seemed to Barney that there were two Sam Burkitts instead of one, which, in Barney's considered opinion, were two too many.

"Burkitt," growled Barney. He said the name almost like a curse word.

The tall, bearded man paid no attention. It was one of the many thinks about Sam Burkitt that riled Barney. It was as though Barney just didn't exist in Sam's well-ordered world.

"You been drinkin' a lot, Barney," warned Baldy, one of the bartenders. "Please don't start no trouble." He quickly held up a defensive hand. Barney never hesitated to hit anyone who disagreed with him, providing he knew the man was unarmed. "Them ain't my words, Barney," said Baldy quickly. "Your old man was in here not too long ago. He knew Burkitt was here too, and he figured you'd be showing up sometime. He told me to warn you not to start trouble if you was to come in. I done it."

Barney downed his third whiskey. He wiped his loose mouth both ways with the back of a hand. "So, you

done your duty. So now shut up and leave me alone."
He slanted his green eyes toward Burkitt. "What's that
mealy-mouthed Law and Order man doing here in a Grant
saloon with all the naughty people of Pawnee?" he asked
truculently.

"He was in your old man's office while Ned was here,"
replied Baldy.

"Complainin' again, I suppose?" said Barney.

"How would I know?"

"What other reason would he have to come in here?
He's *always* complainin'."

"He's a good man, Barney," said the barkeep incau-
tiously. "He just don't think things are right here in
Pawnee. Now I . . ." His voice died away as he saw the
look in Barney's cold bottle-green eyes.

Barney leaned quickly across the mahogany, knocking
over the whiskey bottle. He grabbed the bartender by the
front of his white shirt, twisting it quickly and drawing the
little man closer to his own whiskey-flushed face.

"You sonofabitch!" he snarled. "What the hell do you
mean? Burkitt doesn't *think* things is being run right
here in Pawnee." His voice carried clearly along the
crowded bar. Sam Burkitt slowly lowered his whiskey
glass. He wasn't afraid of Barney Grant. In fact, he was
afraid of no man, including Ned Grant.

Barney shoved Baldy back. "Now you tell that one-
armed, bearded sonofabitch he ain't welcome to drink
here in the Bella Union! Tell him to get the hell out'a
here! The way *he* thinks, he shouldn't be allowed in here
at all!"

Baldy walked along behind the bar. "Go get Ned," he
said out of the side of his mouth to Charley, one of the
two other bartenders. Charley walked to the far end of
the bar to duck under it.

"Where you goin', Charley?" called out Barney.

"To the can," Charley called back.

Barney shook his head. "You can hold it for now," he said.

"You don't have to tell me to leave, Barney," said Sam Burkitt quietly. "I was going on my own anyway."

Millard Forbes, the local druggist, moved toward Barney. He was a Law and Order man, too, and a close friend of Sam Burkitt. "Sam wasn't bothering anybody," he said.

Sam looked at Forbes. He shook his head. "You don't have to make excuses for me," he said. "I was just leaving anyway." He started to walk slowly toward the batwings.

"Yella, one-armed bastard," mouthed-off Barney as Sam passed him.

Sam Burkitt stopped and slowly turned to look at Barney. Barney got nervous under the frosty, blue-eyed stare of the older man. "Don't you pull no gun on me, Burkitt!" he blustered.

Ory Phillips, the local liveryman, came along the bar. "The man can stay here if he wants to, Barney," he said. Ory was a gutsy man who took no lip from anyone, especially Barney Grant. "This is a public place," he added.

Barney spat at Ory's feet. "Keep out'a this, you," he coldly warned. "You're another one of them Law and Order pups, ain't you?"

Ory stuck out his chin. "Sure am, mister!"

Barney backhanded Ory across the face. Ory staggered backward, reaching inside his coat for his double-barreled Derringer. It was a bad mistake. Men in the line of fire broke to get out of the way. Barney, drunk or sober, was a creditable fast-draw artist. He slapped his hand down for the draw and cleared leather, hooking his thumb over the big spur hammer of the Colt, whipped it up and let the weight of the pistol cock the hammer. As soon as it was on a level with Ory Phillips' chest Barney squeezed the hairtrigger. Flame and smoke spat out toward the liveryman. The shock of the soft lead .44/40 slug drove Ory backward as it struck his chest and heart. As he went down his right arm was outflung with the hand gripping the cocked stingy gun. The Derringer trigger was pressed in a spasmodic reaction and the .41 slug struck Baldy the bartender in the right eye, dropping him to the duckboards behind the bar. He was dead before he hit them.

Sam Burkitt closed in on Barney. The younger man whirled, held the Colt at hip level and fanned it as fast as he could, driving five slugs into a space a man could cover with the palm of his hand in the center of Burkitt's chest, driving the man backward to crash through the batwings and out onto the wet plank sidewalk.

"Get that drunken sonofabitch!" yelled a Law and Order man. A Grant man slammed a chair down atop his head, fracturing his skull.

Barney flipped open the loading gate of his Colt and quickly ejected the six hot, smoking brass hulls onto the floor. He crammed in six fresh cartridges and snapped shut the loading gate.

"Get Ned Grant!" yelled Charley the bartender.

Barney stood there grinning in the drifting gunsmoke, his Colt held ready, waiting for the next damned fool to rush him. He was in his prime element—trouble.

"Get Bert Quinn!" yelled someone.

A pistol muzzle pressed against the belly of a pro-Grant man exploded, driving the man backward and setting fire to his vest and shirt.

Sheriff Quinn had been across the street on his way to the Bella Union. He came in through the batwings, Colt at hip level, half-cocked and ready for business, fully expecting to be met by a hail of lead or a thrown bottle. He went into action with professional skill, slapping the extra-long barrel of the Colt right and left indiscriminately, until half a dozen buffaloed men lay unconscious on the bloody floor.

"Who the hell started this?" yelled Bert Quinn. "Who the hell was damned fool enough to kill Sam Burkitt?"

"It was Barney Grant!" yelled a Law and Order man.

Bert Quinn looked down at Ory Phillips, lying dead at his feet, staring up at him with eyes that did not see. He had always liked Ory Phillips. He glanced toward the bat-wings where he could see the soles of Sam Burkitt's big shoes. He looked at the smoking Colt in Barney's hand and then up into Barney's dull, red-rimmed green eyes. For months he had been expecting something like this to happen and he had warned Ned Grant about it time and time again, but Grant, though he would almost always listen to Bert's good advice, could never see any wrong in his only son. "He's a lot like his mother," he would say when someone complained about Barney. "A little wild. He'll cool down one of these days." But Ned Grant could not admit what Sam Burkitt and Bert Quinn could so plainly see—times were changing in Pawnee, Harker County, the state of Kansas and, in fact, the entire West. They were changing for the better. There was no longer any place in Western society for men like Ned and Barney Grant.

Barney grinned loosely. "Yuh gonna lock me up, Bert?" he sneered. He laughed as he turned and reached for the nearest whiskey bottle. The long barrel of Quinn's Colt hit Barney on the side of his thick skull before he could close his hand on the bottle.

"Jesus, Bert, you done it now," breathed Charley.

"Oh, my God," said Anson Crowder, the local justice of the peace, notary public and another Grant man. "You could have run him in without doing *that,* Bert."

Bert reached down, plucked Barney's Colt from his hand and placed it on the bar. He looked about at the watching faces. "Fact is," he said quietly, "I got a lot of satisfaction out of doing it." He reached down and hooked a big, powerful hand under Barney's gun belt and half-carried, half-dragged the unconscious young man through the batwings, across the plank boardwalk and into the muddy, puddled street. He dragged Barney through the puddles and the piles of wet manure to the sheriff's office across the wide street and hauled him inside.

"Someone go get Ned," said Anson Crowder.

"He ain't goin' to like this," said Charley.

Crowder grinned. "If it wasn't for the killings, I would think it was damned funny," he said.

"Ned is over at the hotel," said Charley. He mechanically mopped at the bar, looking away from the sprawled body of his pal. "Ned is over at the hotel," he repeated for lack of anything better to say. He wiped the cold sweat from his face with the bar towel. He had been standing only a few feet away from Baldy when the bullet had struck and killed the other bartender.

Hank Johnson pushed his cards and chips toward the center of the poker table. "You quitting?" asked the dealer. Johnson nodded. "After that? I couldn't keep my mind on cards now."

The dealer shrugged. "There's been a killing at least once a month in the saloons of this burg every year for at least five years. It's part of the night's entertainment. You look like a fighting man, mister. Shouldn't bother you to see a little blood."

"Not *cold* blood," said Johnson. He took out the makings and began to shape a cigarette. He looked thoughtfully at the body of Ory Phillips and at the groaning stunned men who were sitting up, holding their bleeding heads. They had gone down like trees before a hurricane under the brutal Colt barrel of Bert Quinn. "Quinn is quite a man at buffaloing," he added quietly. He ran his tongue along the edge of the cigarette paper. "He even looked like he was enjoying it."

The dealer expertly stacked the cards together and riffled them. "He surely does. I'd like a gold eagle piece for every man Quinn has laid low with that damned Colt of his. I'd be a wealthy man, mister."

Johnson nodded thoughtfully as he lighted his cigarette. He passed his left hand slowly through the thick graying hair at the side of his head to feel the faint ridged scar hidden there. Bert Quinn's hard Colt barrel had laid open *his* scalp to the bone some ten years past when Quinn had seen to it that Hank Johnson had gone to the state pen on a rigged charge. Quinn had then just recently taken over as sheriff of Harker County. He had been a fairly honest man before then; at least as honest as most political appointees.

"You're new around here, ain't you?" asked the dealer as he studied Hank.

Hank Johnson nodded.

"Traveling man?"

"Buffalo hunter," said Hank.

"Not much of that left anymore since the railroads came in and the buffalo hunters killed off the buffalo and put the Indians out of business. Now it's all cattlemen around here."

Hank nodded again. "Sure is."

"Seems like I've seen you somewhere before. It was a long time ago, though. Way back, maybe five or ten years." The dealer rubbed his jaw thoughtfully. "This your first time in Pawnee?"

"Yes, it is."

"Well, anyways, he was a much younger man. By that I mean he wouldn't look like you do after ten years. He'd be much younger looking. No offense, friend."

Hank shook his head. He was only thirty years old and looked closer to forty. Ten years in the state pen had been like twenty outside. His youth had vanished in jail, never to return, but the memories and hatred had not been erased. If anything, they had been better nourished while Hank Johnson had festered in prison.

"Hell! I remember now!" cried the dealer. "The name was Hank Johnson. Young fella. Got into trouble with the law here. Bert Quinn laid him low, I tell you. Beat the poor kid into a bloody pulp for him claiming he was the wrong man accused of rustling. You know of Hank Johnson?"

Hank stood up. "No, I never heard of him," he replied. "Likely, I never will hear of him either, mister. Good night."

The dealer watched Hank work his way through the excited crowd, past the swearing men Quinn had beaten, men whose heads were now being bandaged by Doc Tubbs. Other men were carrying the bodies of Ory Phillips, Baldy the bartender and Sam Burkitt into the undertaker's wagon outside the saloon.

"Barney Grant will never get away with this one," said a Law and Order man.

"Sure!" said a cowpoke. "Barney Grant can get away with *anything* so long as he's got that sonofabitch of an old man behind him to back his play. If he hadn't, somebody would'a shot him in the back long before tonight!"

Ned Grant pushed his way past the men carrying the dead bodies and looked wildly about the saloon. "Where the hell is Barney?" he yelled.

"Over in the jail," said a man.

"Is he all right?" demanded Grant.

"He's got a split skull," said Anson Crowder.

"Who did it? One of these men he gunned down?" asked Ned.

Crowder shook his head. "It was Bert Quinn that did it," he replied. He looked away from Ned Grant's hard, cold stare.

Ned's eyes narrowed. "Why? Did the kid draw on Bert?"

No one replied. Men looked away from Ned Grant. He was not too pleasant to look upon or to deal with when his only son was threatened or harmed.

"I asked you a question, Crowder," said Ned quietly.

"Well, Barney didn't exactly draw on him, Ned," replied the justice of the peace. "You see, Barney got a little lippy with Bert, and Bert has been right touchy these past few months, especially about Barney. You know the sheriff. He doesn't take any crap from anyone." Excepting *you*, Crowder thought to himself.

Ned Grant bent his head and looked back and forth, exactly like a mad bull getting ready to charge anybody or anything. Four men came through the batwings one after the other and ranged themselves behind Ned. Every man in the saloon except quiet Hank Johnson knew who they were. They were the nucleus, the very heart and core of Ned Grant's lawless *corrida* of outlaws, gunslingers, crooked gamblers and other hardcases who swore allegiance to Ned Grant, and his payroll.

Cass Barker was a smiling, affable young killer, once known as the Laredo Kid, but now simply called the Kid. He looked like an altar boy but he could kill with the speed and accuracy of a diamondback rattler and with as little emotion. Monk Cole, a burly, squat giant of a man, more square than high, was a human automaton who obeyed Ned Grant's orders to the letter. He wasn't too bright, but he was the strong-arm member of the quartet. Some claimed he had once killed an ox by hitting it with his fist between its eyes. No one could remember anyone who challenged and fought Monk Cole and came out of the conflict less than maimed, and more often beaten to death. Monk had left a trail of beaten, crippled and dead men behind. Sid Kellar was a quiet, fairly well-educated expert in weapons and explosives. He lived only for his work, taking a professional interest in it. Mark Manton, a tall, dark-haired man, graying at the temples, who

sported an imperial beard and mustache, was a former
Confederate soldier who had fought for Maximilian of
Mexico rather than take the oath of allegiance to the
United States after the war. He had fought in half a dozen
revolutions in Mexico and in the Banana Republics. If
Fate had ever managed to allow Mark Manton to serve on
the winning side in any conflict in which he had partici-
pated he would have achieved fame and glory and had his
name in history books. He was hard, brilliant, and erratic.
As it was, he was really a loser, but with a diamond-
sharp mind which he used to carry out Ned Grant's sur-
reptitious and lawless operations. He was the acknowledged
leader of the Four Horsemen, as the quartet was known
in Pawnee and Harker County.

Hank Johnson stood in the background studying Grant
and his Four Horsemen. He had heard of these men
while he was in the pen. They had been looked upon
with respect and awe by the other cons. Most of all, the
cons had looked up to Ned Grant for his matchless ability
to handle such men. It took a man's man to do it and Ned
Grant was very much that. The fifth gear in Ned Grant's
political and economic empire was Sheriff Bert Quinn,
although ostensibly he was the law and order in the
county. There wasn't any question but that the Four
Horsemen, as well as the rest of his big *corrida,* backed
Ned Grant's crooked dealings, but Bert Quinn, while not
obviously doing so, gave Ned Grant control of the county
law. Therefore, thought Hank Johnson, anyone who dealt
with Grant and his Four Horsemen would have Bert
Quinn to deal with, and vice-versa, and that was Hank
Johnson's major problem on his trail of vengeance against
Bert Quinn. He had nothing against Grant and his *corrida,*
but they would be in his way when he brought Quinn to a
bloody accounting. It was a strong hand to beat—a full
house.

Hank signaled for a drink from the end of the bar

where Barney had been laid low. He watched Ned Grant leave the Bella Union, closely trailed by his four men. Hank had come all the way to Pawnee for one purpose alone: to confront Bert Quinn and let the aging lawman know why he had come, and then to shoot it out with him, hoping to be his executioner rather than again being his victim as he had been ten years earlier. He had managed to survive those ten years of hell by keeping alive the bittersweet thought of revenge on Bert Quinn, aided by his intense hatred of the sheriff and all he stood for in Pawnee and Harker county.

It didn't really matter to Hank what might happen to him if he did execute Bert Quinn. Quinn must and would pay for the ten years lost from Hank's life. That was all that really mattered. Hank Johnson was a thoroughly dedicated man.

Hank sipped his liquor, idly watching the swamper mopping up the blood from the saloon floor and then covering it with sand. Hank's major problem was how to get around Ned Grant and his Four Horsemen to get at Bert Quinn. It would be one against six, in truth; six of the toughest hardcases Hank had ever seen, including those in the state pen.

Hank looked at the shaken Charley. "What will happen to Bert Quinn?" he asked.

Charley shrugged. "Quinn ain't afraid of Ned Grant. Oh, he respects Ned Grant's position here in Pawnee and the county, but I can't say that he's afraid of him."

Hank looked over his shoulder almost as though he could see the confrontation of Grant and Quinn. Maybe Grant would beat Hank out in the cause of killing Quinn. There was nothing Hank could do about it now, in any case.

"You're new around here, ain't you?" asked Charley.

Hank nodded. Strangers seemed to be pretty obvious in Pawnee.

"Helluva welcome for a stranger," observed Charley.

Hank smiled. "Oh, I don't know. I heard Pawnee had a killing *every* Saturday night."

"Well, it's not as bad as all that, but bad enough," said Charley.

"This Barney that was hauled off to jail. He's a tough nut, eh?"

Charley looked quickly about himself as though someone might be eavesdropping. He leaned closer. "Hell," he said in a low voice. "An average man could take him down easy enough with a corn cob and a lightnin' bug."

"He killed two men in less time than it takes to tell about it," reminded Hank.

"Hell! Ory Phillips was no gunhand and Sam Burkitt was one-armed and never carried a gun, anyway."

"He's Ned Grant's son, ain't he?"

"The only son." Charley rolled his eyes upwards. "Some son," he added. "He certainly ain't no chip off the old block."

"Looks like he might have done it this time. Things will probably go bad now for his old man."

"Not Ned! He runs this town and this country, too! He can cover up for Barney. He always does. Course, Barney never done anything quite as bad as this before. I been expecting it though, and so has everyone else in Pawnee."

"What will happen to Sheriff Quinn?"

Charley polished a glass and held it up to the light to inspect it. "That's what I'm wondering. Quinn is a double-barreled, two-fisted sonofabitch. At least, he's always *been* that way, but lately Ned Grant ain't been too happy with Quinn. Quinn is softening, in *my* opinion, anyway. Maybe his conscience is bothering him. Well, he's over fifty years old, a tough age for a man to carry around like he's been doing for the past twenty years or so, especially these last ten here in Pawnee."

Hank looked into his liquor glass. "Maybe his memories

are crowding in on him late at night when he can't sleep."

Charley looked curiously at the quiet stranger. "Yeah," he said slowly. "A man's apt to find that happening, I guess, especially a man as crooked as Quinn has been, but for Christ's sake, don't ever tell him I said so!"

Hank shook his head. "If I ever get to talk to Bert Quinn it won't be about that. It might be about a memory, though." Hank drained his glass and turned to leave the bar.

"Mister!" called out Charley.

Hank turned.

"Ain't I seen you somewheres before?"

"I doubt it."

"Here, in Pawnee?"

Hank shook his head. "I said it was the first time I've ever been here."

"Well, hope it ain't the last, mister."

Hank nodded. "It just might be," he said quietly. "It just might be at that." He pushed his way through the batwings and walked across the bloody planks where Sam Burkitt had died so suddenly.

Chapter 2

Bert Quinn dragged Barney into a cell and dropped him on the floor. He unbuckled Barney's tooled leather holster and swung it out the door. He locked the cell door behind him and hurried out to the back of the office. He swiftly saddled his gray horse and thrust a Winchester into the saddle scabbard. He led the horse from the shed and tethered it right behind the rear door of the office. He went back inside and filled a canteen with water and a sack with some food. He returned to the horse and hooked the canteen to the saddle and slung the sack over the saddle cantle. He went back into the office and emptied all of the rifles and shotguns racked behind his desk. He dumped the cartridges behind a book-case and then took a ten-gauge double-barreled sawed-off Greener shotgun from the rack and broke it. He loaded it with shells from a box in his desk. He was expecting some visitors—Ned Grant and his Four Horsemen.

"My old man will kill you, you tin-starred sonofabitch," warned Barney from his cell when he came to.

Quinn sat down and turned in his swivel chair. "I should have broken your thick skull, sonny," he said. "You killed two damned fine men tonight. Or doesn't that mean anything to you?"

"Burkitt and Phillips? They weren't my old man's men. Law and Order!" jeered Barney. "All they've ever done is give my old man big trouble. Hell! My old man's been running this town ever since he came out here riding a buckboard with an old army tent in back of it and a couple of cases of booze to start the Bella Union. My old man *is* Pawnee! My old man *is* Harker County! There ain't nobody around here done what he done and they never will!"

"Not the way he did it," Quinn quietly added. He bit off the end of a short six and lighted the weed over the top of the Argand desk lamp cylinder.

"He was the toughest hombre ever come around here, including *you,* mister! He still is! He'll cut you down to size before he kills you for what you done to me."

"Hear! Hear!" Quinn exclaimed. He eyed the sullen-faced, half-drunk young man. "You ever take stock of yourself, Barney?"

"What the hell do you mean?"

"Look at yourself! How old are you? Twenty? Twenty years old and you haven't worked an honest day in your whole score of years."

"I don't have to!"

"You will some day. Your old man won't last forever."

Barney narrowed his little eyes. "What are you driving at, Quinn?" he asked.

"What happens when your old man goes? His time is coming. Make sure of that, sonny. A shot out of the dark. A knife in the back. A shot through the head from a dry gulch. The ways are many, and they are sure, and they will come to him, as they do to all men like him. Live by the sword and ye shall die by the sword."

"You been drinking? You're talkin' funny."

"I'm a comedian, Barney. Go on! Tell me what your plans are when your old man leaves this vale of tears?" Quinn asked.

"Supposing I tell you personally, Bert?" replied Ned

Grant from the front doorway. He walked toward the desk and stood in front of it looking down at the sheriff.

Bert Quinn slowly turned his chair. "Do," he politely invited.

Mark Manton, Sid Kellar, Monk Cole and the smiling Laredo Kid walked quietly in behind their boss, coldly watching Bert Quinn.

Slowly, *ever* so slowly, Bert placed his right hand on the grip of the shotgun he held on his lap. It pointed directly at about Ned Grant's knee level, and the muzzle was only a foot or so from his legs.

"Now," said Ned quietly, *very* quietly, "supposing you tell me exactly what the hell you thought you were doing back in the Bella Union when you nearly killed my son?"

"I'm all right now, Pa!" Barney called out.

"He killed two good men, for no reason whatsoever, seemed to me, Ned," Quinn said.

"They started the fight!" shrilled Barney.

"Is that right, Bert?" asked Ned.

"I wasn't there."

Grant nodded. "Exactly. You *weren't* there." His point was very clear.

"Ory Phillips was no gunman," argued Bert in a losing cause. "Sam Burkitt, a one-armed man, never carried a gun to my knowledge. Not since the day he lost his arm at Gettysburg."

"I say they started the fight," insisted Barney.

"Well?" Grant asked Quinn.

Bert jerked a thumb back toward his loud-mouthed prisoner. "I've been sick of that damned drunkard back there for months. He swaggers up and down Grant Street like he owns it, booting anyone around he doesn't take a fancy to. He's pistol-whipped several bartenders because they wouldn't serve him drinks because he was drunk, and *they* were only obeying your orders, Grant. The whores are scared to death of him. Shall I tell you what he did to one of them just last week?"

Ned cut an impatient hand sideways. "Shut up! I don't want to hear anymore lies from you, Quinn! You had no real cause to buffalo my boy tonight!"

"Well, after all, he had just murdered two men practically in cold blood," said Bert quietly. "Maybe you're right at that."

Ned looked sideways, both ways, into the hard faces of his four waiting men. He looked down at Bert Quinn. "Your time is over here in Harker County. For months you've been falling down on the job. You've even been favoring the Law and Order party around here."

Bert nodded. "After all, Ned, I *am* the sheriff here. The day will soon be here when they'll take over and run the lot of us out of Pawnee."

"You *were* the sheriff," corrected Ned.

"You can't fire me," Quinn bluffed. "I am a duly elected county officer."

"Listen to him," sneered Mark Manton. "Let me and the boys teach him some manners, Ned."

Ned shook his head. "I want to hear the rest of this," he said. "I can't believe my own ears."

Bert unpinned his badge with his left hand, making sure that his right hand was ready for action, the trigger finger resting on the first trigger of the Greener. He tossed the badge down in front of Grant. "It's yours," he said. "I'm leaving Pawnee tonight. Forever . . ."

Ned Grant looked down at the star. "What makes you think so?" he asked quietly. He raised his head and his eyes seemed to bore into Quinn's eyes. "You know too much, Bert. I can't afford to have you leave."

"I've resigned," said Bert.

Ned shook his head. "No one resigns from my organization, Quinn. Not even you."

"Before you kill him, Pa," shrilled Barney, "you buffalo

him good! Better yet, let *me* do it, Pa! I'll beat the sense out of that thick head of his!"

It was very quiet in the room.

No one moved.

The clock's ticking suddenly became more noticeable.

Bert Quinn eased his left hand over to the shotgun and pushed back the hammers, fully cocking them. The sharp double-clicking sound was heard loud and clear by Ned Grant and his four men.

Bert smiled a little, just at the corners of his wide mouth below his thick dragoon mustache. "Now, Ned, before your executioners there can make a move toward a gun, or me, I can cut you down at knee level with one charge from this shotgun and kill you with the other one before you hit the floor. Do I make myself clear?"

The five hard men looked down at the one hard man who sat, seemingly at ease, and in full control of the situation, behind his desk. They knew he'd do exactly as he said he would.

"What is it you want, Quinn?" asked Ned quietly. He hated to do it. God, how he hated to do it!

Bert smiled a little. "I aim to leave Pawnee tonight, forever, like I said. But, I'm not stupid enough to do any talking about you and Pawnee and your rotten little kingdom here in Harker County, Grant. I'd only implicate myself and that wouldn't be very smart, now would it?" Bert never took his eyes from Ned's eyes, waiting for that fraction of a second giveaway before a man could go into deadly action. It did not come.

Bert stood up slowly, raising the shotgun until it was level with Ned Grant's belly. His cold blue eyes held Ned's green ones. "Now, you gentlemen just put your holster guns and your hideout guns right there on the desk in front of me. Carefully!"

Colts and Derringers were piled on the desk. Bert opened a desk drawer and swept the lot into it with his left hand. He locked the drawer and put the key into a shirt pocket. "None of the Winchesters or the shotguns in the rack behind me are loaded," he said. "The cartridges are hidden. Now, I've got a good horse saddled outside the jail in the alleyway. I'd ask for half an hour's start but you'd never give it to me. So, by the time you get to your guns and your horses I'll have at least twenty minutes start in the darkness and you don't know where I'm heading."

The clock ticked steadily away as the five men looked at Bert Quinn.

"You gonna let him get away with this, Pa?" demanded Barney.

"Have you got any better ideas?" asked Ned.

Bert backed slowly and carefully past the row of cells to the rear door of the office, keeping the shotgun pointed toward the five men. He opened the door with one hand behind himself and then quickly jumped outside and slammed the door shut turning the key in the lock. He loosed his big gray horse and hit the saddle with a smashing of wet leather. He slapped the butt of the Greener across the rump of the horse and sank in his spurs. The gray took off down the alleyway like a Comanche arrow shot from a sinew-backed bow. In a few minutes, Bert Quinn was lost in the rainy darkness.

Chapter 3

Ned Grant stood at the window of his hotel suite in the Grant Hotel, looking down on muddy Grant Street, with a Grant Stogie clenched in his mouth. Behind him, seated around a large marble-topped table were the Four Horsemen: Mark Manton, Sid Kellar, the Laredo Kid and Monk Cole, silently watching their boss. Bluish tobacco smoke filled the big room and drifted slowly toward the partly opened windows. Now and then glass clinked as one or the other of the Four Horsemen sipped at Ned Grant's fine booze, labeled Grant's Special Blend.

"I still say we can't risk using Barney on the Dodge City Bank job," argued Mark Manton. "It will be risky enough for the four of us, Ned."

"I think we need five men," said Grant stubbornly over his shoulder. "It was *me* that thought up this job. It was *me* that explained it to you four. It's *me* who's going to say how many men are in on it, and *who* that fifth man will be!"

"But not Barney," insisted Mark.

Ned turned slowly. "Look," he said quietly. "I know the damned fool started that ruckus in the Bella Union and killed the two top Law and Order men. I thought it would blow over, but a month has already passed and there are no signs of its blowing over. It's still the main topic of conversation in Pawnee. It just won't die! Any day now I expect to have someone find Barney with a bullet hole in the back of his head or a knife in his back and I couldn't stand that!"

"Can't Lem Martin keep things under control?" asked Sid Kellar.

Ned shook his head. "He's a good man for sheriff, at least here in Harker County." Here he allowed himself a slight smile, which was immediately reflected in the hard faces of the Four Horsemen. Ned Grant rarely exhibited any humor, so it was wise and politic to recognize it when he did. "But, he ain't any Bert Quinn, at least the *oldtime* Bert Quinn," added Grant.

"But it's Barney who's the thorn in the side of the Law and Order group, and the *good* citizens of Pawnee. They outnumber us now, men, by three to one. The only advantage we have over them now is organization, and we also hold the economic and political power here, so we are still top dog. But it's this mess Barney got us into that's tilting the scales. The people of Pawnee want Barney arrested and brought to trial. That's why I want him out of town, maybe permanently, depending on how this Dodge City job comes through. That depends on you four, *and* Barney."

"It's too tricky," insisted Mark. "Each of us knows exactly what to do. We're a team, Ned. The best in the business."

Ned nodded. "Granted, but you still need five men to do this job. It's big! It's the biggest thing ever planned in this state. Maybe in the whole West!" His eyes got a little wild. He has been showing signs of irrationality for some time, thought Mark.

None of the four wanted Barney on the Dodge City job. None of the four had any use for him. In fact, each one of the four hated Barney's guts. Besides, there was far too much at stake on the projected robbery of the Dodge City Bank.

Ned sat down and poured himself a Grant's Special.

He relighted his Grant's Stogie over the Argand lamp cylinder. He leaned back in his chair. "Look," he said. "I hate like hell to have to ask you four boys to take Barney along with you. I can *order* you to take him, but I don't want it that way. Look, he's got to start learning the basics of my business. I won't be around forever, and the way he is now, he doesn't know how to take care of the small fortune I'm going to leave to him in money, business and real estate. Fact is, my entire fortune is wrapped up in this damned town. Can you imagine what would happen to Barney if anything happened to me? I can handle these Law and Order yokels just by being around here backed by my *corrida* and Lem Martin, but Barney wouldn't last five minutes. Can't you see that?"

"Too bad," Monk Cole drily whispered sideways to the Kid.

Ned leaned forward. "Also, things may soon be coming to a head here in Pawnee and Harker County. State and federal authorities are getting curious about a lot of things going on around here."

"What's your angle?" asked Sid Kellar.

Ned looked back over both shoulders as though someone might be watching them. He got up and padded lightly to the door, opening it quickly and looking both ways up and down the long carpeted hallway.

Mark Manton shrugged. The Kid rolled his blue eyes upwards. Sid Kellar shook his head. Monk Cole yawned; he was bored.

Ned came back to the table. *"Mexico!"* he said. "With the money from the Dodge City Bank raid we can grease the palms of the officials down in Coahuila and buy up a damned area the size of an American county. We can live like *hacendados* down there! Like *kings!*" He looked about at the four silent men. They had never seen him quite like this before.

"Haven't you got enough money here in Pawnee?"

asked Mark. "This will be a risky deal, Ned. After all, Dodge isn't like Pawnee, and they've got that damned tin-starred thief-killer Matt Dillon sitting down there just waiting for people like us."

"Dillon is chicken," sneered the Kid.

Mark looked quickly at him. "You talk like a damned fool!" he snapped. "You don't know the man at all!"

The Kid grinned, "I'd like to try him."

"That's not our purpose," said Mark.

Sid Kellar lit a cigarette. He looked up at Ned. "How much do you estimate will be in the Dodge City Bank?" he asked.

"At the right time, what with the railroad payroll, cattle buyers' money, and some forthcoming property sales in and around the town, on which I have inside information, I figure there will be between $200,000 and $250,000 in the vault."

"Jesus," said Monk Cole softly.

"You're sure about that, Boss?" asked the Kid.

Mark nodded. "He's sure," he said. "He's always sure in deals like this one. That's why he's where he is today. You can copper that bet, Kid."

"I've been looking into this deal for over a year, getting information on bank deposits, loan money, payroll money and so on from banks in Phillipsburg, Hays, Larned, Scott City and Liberal, to name a few of them. It so happens that right about this time, Dodge will have the biggest sum. It just worked out that way," continued Ned Grant.

"It's still a helluva risk," said Mark. He looked down at the street map of Dodge City he and Ned had worked out.

"Look, Mark," said Ned. "I've laid all the groundwork. I've figured out which bank will have the greatest amount of money at any given time. I figured out the strategy; you figured out the tactics. As a team, we're the best in the business. How the hell can we go wrong?"

"Dillon," said Mark. It was all he had to say. He looked up from the chart into Ned's hard green eyes.

"Supposing he isn't there when you make the hit?" softly asked Ned.

"Go on," urged Mark.

"I've worked out a plan to get him out of town. I intend to call Bill Gaines, the Dodge City Bank president, up here on business. That means that the two prime men who might wreck your raid won't be there that night. What more could you want?"

The Kid shaped a quirly. "Why bother with Dodge at all, Boss? Why don't we make our hit right here, get your money out of here, meet you in Mexico and live like kings?" He grinned.

Ned Grant leaned back in his chair. "Because there isn't that much cash money of mine here now in Pawnee," he quietly replied. "My money is tied up in real estate and in my businesses. It's frozen, Kid. Besides, any day now the state and federal authorities may make an audit of my books and they may find some big discrepancies. I've already invested money in down payments in Coahuila in preparation for you boys and myself going down there. You understand now, Kid?"

The Kid nodded as he lit up. "The only thing I still don't understand is why we have to take Barney along. No offense to you, Boss, but it's a helluva risk."

Ned slapped a hand down hard on the table top. "Because I damned well say so! Does that answer your question?" He got to his feet and walked quickly to the window to look out and brood over muddy Grant Street.

Mark Manton looked casually at the Kid. He slanted his gray eyes toward Ned, without Ned seeing him do so, and then nodded, as though to get the Kid to agree to take Barney along after all. He looked at Sid and Monk. "We take him," he whispered.

"All right," said the Kid. "We'll take him along, Boss."

Ned came back to the table. "Why the sudden change of heart?" he asked suspiciously.

Mark looked up at him. "You may be right about Barney, Ned," he said. "Besides, you thought up the idea. You've got a right to say who goes along." He looked away from Ned and slowly winked at Sid Kellar.

They had never seen Ned Grant like this before. The man, usually as cool as a springhouse, was on edge. Suddenly things were not going right for him in Pawnee. Fate was evidently starting a downhill slide for Ned Grant and his Harker County empire. Grant had the ugly feeling that the handwriting on the wall was meant for him.

"When do we make the hit?" asked Mark. "It will have to be on an early Sunday morning."

"A week from tomorrow."

"That soon?"

"They will begin to dole out the money starting Monday morning. Besides, the quietest time of the week is early Sunday morning. Even in Dodge City."

"Rather short notice to break Barney in on the deal."

"The boy will catch on. He's smart as a whip once he puts his mind to it."

"He sure is," said Sid Kellar drily.

Ned Grant walked to the door. He looked back at the four men. "I'll go get Barney and explain to him why it's in his best interests to go along with you boys. Just occupy the time going over the plan again with a fine-tooth comb. I want all the wrinkles to be out of the plan this coming week. Understand?"

"Anything you say, Boss," the Kid agreed.

"Right," said Monk.

Sid Kellar waved a hand.

Mark Manton nodded.

The door closed behind Ned Grant.

As soon as the catch clicked all four of the men looked at each other.

"Jesus," said Monk. "That goddamned punk ain't got the brains to pound sand down a rat hole!"

"I'll back that," said Sid.

The Laredo Kid rolled his blue eyes upwards. "My God," he breathed. He imitated perfectly Ned Grant's brusque, authoritative mode of speech: "The boy will catch on. He's as smart as a whip once he puts his mind to it."

"Once he puts his mind to it," echoed Sid. "When will *that* be? When does he put his mind to anything but drinking and whoring?"

The Kid looked curiously at Mark. "What made you suddenly change your mind, Mark?" he asked.

Mark lit a cigar, looking at the Kid over the flame of the lucifer. "You know the plan," he said. "We make the hit, get the loot, separate, with me taking the loot, and we scatter in five different directions to throw off pursuit. I take the money and cache it. Then I take off east, heading for Larned, circling back around Dodge, headed for Indian Territory. The four of us rendezvous in Texas within a month where we wait for Ned Grant. Grant meets us there with the money, we ride into Mexico and start life anew." He smiled. "You all follow me?"

"I think so," said Monk.

Sid nodded.

"Go on," said the Kid.

"Any questions?" asked Mark.

The Kid looked suddenly at Mark. "What's to prevent Grant from picking up the cached loot and taking off like a striped-assed bird, leaving us sitting down in Mexico like a bunch of hungry crows on a cornfield fence?"

"That's a good question," agreed Mark. He looked about the table.

"Yeah," softly said Monk.

"I've been thinking about that," said Sid.

"So, what's your new angle with Barney?" asked the Kid.

Mark leaned forward. "Simply this," he said *sotto voce*. "If we have Barney with us, say in your hands, Sid, or Monk, or the Kid for that matter, after I cache the loot, then Ned has to show up with the money, or Barney gets it from us."

"Brilliant," said Sid.

"Smart," agreed the Kid.

"Jesus," said Monk slowly. "I'da never thought of *that*."

Mark leaned back in his chair. "There are some catches, however. The first one is taking that drunken idiot with us on a tricky raid like this one. We'll have to watch him every minute to see that he doesn't blow it for us. Secondly, are we sure Ned cares so much about his only kid to come across with the loot at the right time?"

The Kid laughed. "I wouldn't," he said.

Mark got up and walked to the door. He opened it and did as Ned had done, looking up and down the hallway. He closed the door and came back to the table. "Don't give Grant the idea we came around to his point of view just like that. The Old Man is too smart to fall for that right off. He's damned suspicious by nature, as you all know. You get me?"

They all nodded.

The Kid scratched in his curly blonde hair. "Hell," he said thoughtfully. "As far as that goes, what's to prevent us from taking the loot for ourselves and bag-assing for Mexico and to hell with the Old Man *and* Barney?"

"We aren't the *only* ones working for Ned Grant," quietly replied Mark. "He's got a long arm, the Boss has. He can reach clear down to Mexico, or maybe even South America, to get us, and you'd better be damned sure he can—and will—do just that. He's no fool. He's probably worked out that eventuality in any case."

The Kid suddenly raised his head. "Someone's coming," he announced. He had hearing like a Chiricahui Apache.

"Then it's agreed?" asked Mark. "We take his baby boy along for the ride. We'll have to herd him along and watch him like hawks to see that he doesn't blow up the whole plan but, in a way, having him along will be like a form of insurance."

"Life insurance," added Sid Kellar drily.

Ned Grant opened the door and came in, trailed by a shambling, hungover Barney. Barney yawned. "Helluva time to do this," he complained.

"It's six o'clock," said Mark.

"In the evening," added Sid.

"Nobody asked you!" snapped Barney.

Ned placed a chair for Barney who breathed sour whiskey fumes over the table, making the othsrs a little goggle-eyed.

"Go over the plan, Mark," instructed Ned. He sat down and lighted a fresh cigar.

Mark hitched his chair closer to the table and smoothed out the neatly made map of Dodge City and its environs. "We travel separately. Except for me and Barney—we travel together," Mark began. "We meet here at this abandoned farmhouse five miles from the city and across the Arkansas River. The Kid will scout Dodge City a few days before the raid and get the lay of the land, then report to us at the farmhouse. While he's in Dodge, he watches the routines of the marshal's office and the bank and makes sure Dillon and Gaines are out of town. That's damned important!

"Meanwhile, me, Barney, Sid and Monk lay low in the farmhouse. Sid prepares his explosive charges there. Monk makes leather boots for the horses. I've already

arranged for fresh horses for us after we escape from
Dodge so we can outdistance any possible pursuit. Although we original four planned to escape four different ways and alone, I'll take Barney with me back up
east to cache the money, and then he can head for
Mexico with me."

"I'd rather come back here," said Barney stupidly.

"You'll do as Mark says," said his father.

"Each day and evening before the strike, each of us
will go alone into Dodge by turns and get acquainted with
conditions, the street layouts, the general arrangements of
the town, the interior of the bank, and so forth. The Kid
stays in Dodge until early Sunday morning, then reports
to us at the farmhouse if everything is still satisfactory
for the raid. When the Kid reports, we boot the horses,
taking along an extra horse or two. We ride to the plank
bridge. The Kid goes on ahead, cuts the telegraph line
before he goes into the town proper, and takes his post
at a street intersection where he can slow down or stop
any interference in case we are found out." Here Mark
traced a finger on the map along the plank bridge span-
ning the wide Arkansas River, pointed out the telegraph
line, and then the Kid's position in the street.

Mark looked about at the faces, all intent except
Barney's. "Monk and Barney then go in and make sure
the way to the bank is clear. If there's any killing to be
done, it has to be done silently."

Monk nodded. "You can count on me," he said.

Barney yawned.

"Monk covers the front of the marshal's office and the
street intersection there, as well as the front of the bank.
Barney will cover the rear of the marshal's office and the
alleyway behind the bank, as well as that street intersection. Sid and I come across the bridge, Sid plants his
explosives under the middle of the bridge and places his
fuse. We lead the horses to the rear of the bank. Then Sid

sets squib charges to blow off the door hinges. They're not very loud and it'll be three o'clock on a Sunday morning, so the chances of them being heard are not too good.

"Once the rear door is blown we enter the bank. I cover Sid while he blows the vault door. When the vault is blown the whole town will wake up, but it will be a good ten to fifteen minutes before anyone starts for the bank. If there's any trouble from the marshal's office from the front door area, Monk will take care of it; Barney will still be covering the rear of the office. The Kid can slow down anyone coming from other directions. No one in town will be organized like we are, eh?" Mark smiled.

"We'll work fast inside the bank, stowing the money in tow sacks. We leave by the rear door, leading the extra horses. Once we're near the bridge, Monk and Barney follow along, with the Kid as rear guard. Can't think of a better one, eh, Kid?"

The Kid grinned. "The best," he said.

"I get across the bridge first with the loot. Sid waits until Monk, Barney and the Kid cross and then he blows the middle out of the damned bridge. He comes ashore. I take off with Barney to the east. You others know your retreat routes and where the fresh horses are held for you. That's it, boys."

Ned Grant nodded. "Show Barney his post," he suggested.

Mark pointed out the alleyway and its intersection with the street. Barney blinked in a bored way at it. Mark wasn't even sure Barney could focus on it.

"You see it, Barney?" asked his father.

"Jeeesuss," murmured Barney. "Supposing Dillon comes outa there loaded for bear and sees ol' Barney standing there? Man, I'd like to see that sonofabitch draw on *me!*"

"He won't be there," said Mark.

"Well, he might be," admitted Ned. "We can't be too

sure. But Barney will take care of him," he hopefully added.

"You'd better believe it!" crowed Barney, suddenly all horns and rattles. "Sonofabitch! Any man as could gun down Matt Dillon on his own ground, right in Dodge there, would be the kingpin of the whole damned State of Kansas, now wouldn't he?"

Mark Manton looked sideways at Barney. "That's not the idea," he reminded Barney. "We don't want any more killing than we can help. None at all would be best. If we fail, we'd only be held for attempted bank robbery. If we kill anyone and fail, it'll be a big barbecue and a necktie party for us. Just remember that, Barney."

"Bull!" snapped Barney. "You're goin' to make a go of it now that you got *me* interested in it. Why, if Dillon or anyone else gets bumped off, we'll be on our way out of Kansas so goddamned fast the flies won't have time to settle on us!"

"Sure will," said Sid Kellar drily.

"It's agreed then?" asked Ned Grant. He wasn't really asking them; he was telling them.

Mark avoided Ned's searching eyes. He nodded.

"Sid?" asked Grant.

"All right with me."

"Monk?"

"Sure."

"Kid?"

The Kid grinned. "With Barney along, how can we fail?" he asked lightly.

Grant searched the Kid's guileless face and then he looked at his son. "You take your orders from Mark, you hear? Stay off the booze. After this hit you can swim in the damned stuff for all I care, but you stay sober until this deal is over. You understand?"

Barney nodded sourly.

Mark folded the map and placed it inside his coat.

"I'll spread the word that you're all riding north on a little job for me," said Ned. "I've arranged for a telegram, supposedly from Mark here, to be sent from Phillipsburg the same day you'll be making the hit. That telegraph operator here is a stool-pigeon to the state authorities. The only reason I let him stay on is to receive phoney messages to throw them off the track."

They all stood up. Ned filled the whiskey glasses, carefully avoiding giving a drink to Barney. "Well," he said cheerily, for him, "Here's to success!"

They drank, wiped their mouths, and reached for their hats. The Four Horsemen walked to the door. "See you in Mexico, Ned," said Mark Manton over his shoulder. He closed the door behind himself.

Barney eyed the whiskey bottle.

"No," said Ned Grant firmly to his son. He lit a fresh Grant Stogie and walked to the window. He looked down on Grant Street. "You want to know why I really wanted you to go along, son?" he asked over his shoulder.

"Because they need a good gun like me?" asked Barney eagerly.

Ned shook his head. "I want you to keep an eye on them. This is your big chance. You've got to prove to me that you can handle a deal like this. Understand?"

Barney nodded. He slid his little eyes sideways toward the tempting bottle of Grant's Special.

Ned hooked his thumbs into the armholes of his vest and teetered back and forth on his heels. "You know, son," he said softly, "you're going to be the last man with Mark when he caches the loot. You don't have to continue on with him when he heads for Texas and Mexico. You can come along home here and meet me and we can go back and get the loot and head out of the sovereign State of Kansas."

"What about the others?" asked Barney. For once he had caught on.

Ned turned. "If Mark Manton is dead, you'll be the only one who knows where the loot is cached."

Barney shrugged. "Supposing he don't get killed?"

Ned came closer to him. "Well, then," he said quietly, "maybe you can arrange that, eh, Barney?"

A dull light came into Barney's eyes. "Yeah," he said softly.

"Mexico," said Ned softly. "Romantic Mexico! Music, *señoritas* and a pot full of gold!"

Barney got up and walked to the door. He softly closed the door and headed for the nearest saloon.

Chapter 4

That rainy night when Bert Quinn left Pawnee forever at a steady gallop, he headed for the Saline River Crossing. At dawn on the second morning after his flight he camped in the river breaks and shaved off his trademark dragoon mustache. He made a smokeless fire and heated his coffee and beans. After he had eaten he placed a cracked mirror in a tree crotch and then dyed his salt-and-pepper-colored thatch of hair a medium brown color. He changed his clothes and hid the old clothing under a flat rock. Every now and then, during this process, he peered through the thick brushy areas toward the level country to the south and west looking for pursuit. It wasn't until after nine o'clock that he saw a lone horseman heading for the breaks, riding slowly, evidently following the hoof tracks on the soft ground.

Bert went back to the big gray and withdrew his Winchester '76 from its scabbard. He padded back to the edge of the breaks and rested the rifle barrel in a tree crotch. He levered a round of .50/95 Express into the chamber. He lined up the silver blade front sight in the rear buckhorn sight, allowed a trifle for the fitful, fresh morning wind and squeezed off. The rolling echo of the shot fled across the river beyond the breaks. The horse flung itself sideways and went down, the rider skillfully kicking his feet out of the two stirrups, freeing himself from the horse, and at the same time ripping his rifle

40

from the saddle scabbard. He fired almost as quickly as he readied the rifle and the slug whipped right through the gunsmoke still drifting about Bert Quinn.

Bert crouched and ran through the breaks. He fell belly-flat behind a log, levering in a fresh round of Express, and then thrust the barrel across the log. He could easily kill the man standing there with ready rifle peering toward the gunsmoke, but those days were over for Bert Quinn. All he wanted to do was to slow down and try to stop any possible pursuit. It was enough for Bert Quinn that he had already killed the stranger's horse. Bert squeezed off. The slug whipped past the man's head. He went to earth like a frightened gopher, jumping over his prone horse and thrusting his rifle forward across the saddle to fire at almost the same instant. The slug struck the log and drove soft shards of rain-wet bark against the side of Bert's face. That was enough for him. He ran through the trees and brush to the gray and mounted him, slapping his rump with the butt of the Winchester and heading for the river. He plunged the big gray into the shallow waters and splashed across. By the time he reached the higher ground beyond the Saline he looked back to see a lone figure standing about where Bert's campground was situated. He did not move, seemingly standing motionless, staring at the distant figure of Bert and his big gray.

Bert turned the gray and galloped north and east, heading toward the Solomon River country. It would be quite a while before the stranger could find himself another horse. Maybe he hadn't been trailing Bert, but Bert was taking no chances. Ned Grant's reach was too long to suit him and it would take all of Bert's skill and trickery to keep ahead of Grant's merciless riders.

The gray went down in a deep hollow late in the afternoon. Bert dismounted and unsaddled the horse, whose right front leg was broken. He drew his Colt, cocked it, and shot the horse behind the ear. He hefted his saddle over a shoulder and carried his Winchester, walking five miles to a ranchhouse where he bought a blocky claybank, claiming his horse had broken its leg. He spread the word around at the dinner table that he was heading for the Solomon River country that very night. He rode north and east until he was out of sight of the ranch and then turned sharply southeast and headed for the Saline River again. He rode all that night and by the dawn light, worn by fatigue, he swam the claybank across the Saline and turned back toward the west. By noon he had reached the little hamlet of Walnut Creek with a lame and exhausted horse.

Bert traded off the foundered horse for a solid-looking sorrel with one bad eye, throwing in fifty dollars to boot. He bought a pair of blue-tinted glasses in the local general store, a cheap business suit and a Kansas City hat as well as some food.

In the next twenty-four hours Bert reached Larned, put the sorrel in a livery stable and registered in the hotel. He almost crawled up the stairs to his room, blind with fatigue, and fell onto his bed without taking off his clothing or muddy boots. He lay as one dead for nine straight hours.

"Bill Simpson is the name; selling is the game," Bert told the desk clerk the day he left the hotel, as well as the waitress in the Busy Bee restaurant and the liveryman with whom he had left the sorrel. His eyes sparkled with good humor as he spoke. "Kansas City man," he said. "Best lightning rod salesman west of the Mississippi. Yessir!"

On his way out of town he bought a pair of overalls, a huck coat and a straw hat, and rode due east across the great bend of the Arkansas River until he reached Hutchinson, leaving behind his cheap businessman's suit and hat, and wearing his farmer's outfit. In Hutchinson he hocked his good Winchester rifle, sold the sorrel horse and took the morning train to Wichita. He did not wear his tinted glasses.

In Wichita Bert Quinn looked for work. He was going broke and he found work hard to find. The slow realization came to him that he really didn't know any other kind of work except for being a lawman. He was too old for much else than menial jobs. He knew nothing about cattle and not too much about horses either, for that matter. The railroad was not hiring at the time, and he didn't know a damned thing about railroading, anyway.

"Dodge City is the place for work, mister," said a general storekeeper whom Bert had asked for clerical work. "The place is booming. Railroad work. Cattle drives end there. Plenty of different kinds of businesses. Construction. Any man willing to work can find a job there. Try your luck in Dodge, mister."

Bert Quinn, after repairing the dye job on his hair, got rid of his farmer garb, bought a cheap suit and a secondhand Stetson and bought a ticket for Dodge City with the last of his funds.

Bert stepped off the afternoon train in Dodge, wearing his blue-tinted glasses. He walked slowly through the busy town. The storekeeper in Wichita had been right—Dodge City was a boom town. Heavily laden freight and farm wagons rolled through the dusty streets. The hitching racks were lined with hipshot horses. The sounds of hammering and sawing came from every direction and the whistling of work train locomotives sounded regularly in the distance. The stores were all full and so were the saloons.

Bert stopped across the street from the marshal's office. He leaned against a post and rolled a cigarette. He had known Matt Dillon some years past, and he knew well enough what Dillon's opinion had been of him then, not to mention what it might be currently. But, there was something else to carefully consider—if he wanted to find work in Dodge, he'd never be able to do it incognito while Matt Dillon was marshal there. Bert was far enough away from Pawnee now that maybe, and a long *maybe* it was, Ned Grant might not send anyone after him. Still, it was possible that Grant might reason that Bert would only hurt himself if he talked too much about matters in Harker County. It was well-grounded reasoning.

A cold wind blew down the street, driving dust and old papers ahead of it. Bert turned up his collar and shivered. Winter was coming on fast. He was dead broke and out of work. He turned and looked at himself in a store-window mirror. He walked closer to the mirror and looked at himself honestly for the first time in many years. No longer did he see the tough, hardcase sheriff of Harker County, but rather a man who was already past the prime of his life on the far side of fifty with nothing to show for it. He had no wife, family, true friends or money. There were new lines in his face. His eyes seemed dull behind the blue-tinted glasses. The sharp contrast of his freshly dyed hair to his aging sallow skin and hollowing cheeks made him realize that he hadn't really been fooling anyone but himself.

He threw down his cigarette and stamped on it. He hurriedly crossed the street, threading his way between the wagons, buggies and horses toward Matt Dillon's office before he could change his mind.

Matt Dillon looked up as the burly man with his coat collar turned up came into the office with a blasting of cold air from the outside. The man closed the door behind himself and looked down at Matt through blue-tinted spectacles.

"Can I help you?" Matt politely asked.

Jesus, but he's big and capable-looking, thought Bert

Quinn. A twinge of remorse shot through him. There had been a time in his past, in his early lawman years, when he might have become a lawman such as Matt Dillon. But he had taken the wrong fork in the road ten years before, and now there was no going back.

"Mister?" asked Matt.

"The marshal's talkin' to yuh, mister," put in Festus.

Bert came to a forced alertness with a start. He was cold, tired, dispirited and forcing himself along every inch of the way. "Marshal Matt Dillon?" he asked.

Matt nodded. "I am afraid you have the advantage of me, though."

"I go by the name of Bill Simpson," said Bert.

"You make it sound like it might not be your real name," suggested Matt.

"You know me, Dillon."

Matt shook his head.

Bert took off the glasses. "Take a good look. Every lawman has to have a filing system of names and faces in his memory, especially 'wanted' people."

Matt narrowed his eyes. "You're wanted?"

"Mebbe yuh want to turn yourself in, eh?" suggested Festus.

Matt studied the man: over fifty and in good physical condition for his age although seemingly tired out; hair freshly dyed; faint scar on upper left cheek. He had the look of the manhunter about him. "Bert Quinn," said Matt quietly. "You're a long way from Pawnee and Harker County. And, you're not wanted. Not around here, at least."

Bert smiled crookedly. "Not by you, Dillon."

"Harker County, then?" asked Matt.

Bert shrugged. "In a sense. No formal charges that I know unless Ned Grant has thought some up since I left there in a hurry."

"You were the law up there, as I recall."

Bert shook his head. "I was the instrument of the law, such as it was, if you want to put it that way."

"Manipulated by Ned Grant. Is he still the kingpin up there?"

Bert nodded. "As ever. Some trouble with the Law and Order group. You know how he's run that county and Pawnee ever since he came west after the war."

"Tell me more about this Law and Order group," suggested Matt. He studied Bert. "Is that why you came to Dodge City, Bert?"

"In a way."

"Please set and have some coffee, Mr. Quinn," invited Festus.

"Thanks," said Bert as he sat down. "But please call me Bill Simpson."

"Suits me fine," agreed Festus as he filled three coffee cups.

Bert Quinn, or Bill Simpson, unbuttoned his cheap coat and took off his blue-tinted glasses. "The Law and Order group was started some years past by some of the business and professional men of Pawnee. Pawnee has changed somewhat, Matt, and in some ways not for the best. It's a busy place now. The buffalo hunters and others have given way to farmers and business people. Good money there. Thriving businesses, churches, schools . . . You wouldn't recognize the old place now. I would have liked to have stayed there if it was at all possible, to see its future, but my time there had passed."

"You forgot to mention the saloons, whorehouses, gambling dens and other such savory places," said Matt drily.

Bert took a cup of coffee from Festus' hand. "Well, you can't hardly have a boom camp develop into a town without those places."

"Even Dodge," put in Festus with a grin.

"You can thank Matt Dillon for keeping that situation under control," said Bert.

Matt waved a big hand. "Say rather the good citizens of Dodge and the State of Kansas, Bert. Bill, that is! Without the help of such people a marshal or a sheriff is just another man wearing a star, and he can't ever do it alone. If you haven't got the community behind you, you'll never succeed in this profession."

"I know what you mean," said Bert quietly. "In a sense, that's why I'm here. Ned Grant has become more highhanded. No one can cross him in the slightest thing. Grant is bad enough, but that rat of a son of his has grown up to be the local terror of good, law-abiding citizens."

"I recall him," said Festus. "Little Barney! He was a spoiled punk even then."

Bert looked at him. "Little Barney? He's a grown man now, at least physically. He's a fast gun and a tricky one. He cheats at the gambling tables and gets away with it. He's a terror to the bartenders and whores. Even Ned Grant's own *corrida* can't stand him."

"And the Four Horsemen?" asked Matt. "Are they still riding for Ned Grant?"

"Yes, they're still with him and a terror in their own right, and they're backed by the *corrida*—a bunch of the toughest outlaws and gunslingers in the West. Grant pays them well, gives them privileges and bonuses. They live like fighting cocks and they don't want to see Grant lose his power because that means they'll have to go to prison or find an honest way of life."

"So what brought the situation to a head this time?" asked Matt.

"Who said there was a situation?" asked Bert.

"You don't have to tell me," replied Matt. "You, a man who was the law, legal and illegal, in Harker County for ten years suddenly shows up in Dodge on a cold

fall night wearing cheap clothing, tinted glasses, without
his well-known dragoon mustache, with his graying hair
dyed dark again, and with a convenient change of name,
without there being some situation that forced him to
leave a soft spot like sheriff of Harker County."

Bert shrugged. "All right. You've neatly packaged the
'situation,' as you called it. Barney was on a two-day
drunk. He was in the Bella Union. He started trouble
by insulting Sam Burkitt and another Law and Order
man, Ory Phillips. Burkitt never went armed. He was a
one-armed veteran and a businessman."

"Sort of a local hero to the town, eh?" asked Festus.

"And head of the Law and Order group. Barney
couldn't leave well enough alone. He ordered Burkitt to
leave. Burkitt *was* leaving quietly when Barney called him
a name no man could take. Ory Phillips called Barney
on it. Barney struck him. Phillips made the mistake of
going for his hideout gun and Barney killed him. Burkitt
rushed in to restrain Barney and got five bullets point-
blank through his chest."

"My God," murmured Festus.

"I was called too late," continued Bert. "A bloody
brawl had already broken out in the Bella Union. A bartender had been killed by a stray shot from Phillips' Derringer. Another man had a bullet in his belly. He died
the next day. I came into the saloon and broke up the
fight."

"Alone?" asked Festus.

Bert nodded.

"Bert can do it," said Matt.

Quinn began to shape a cigarette. He seemed preoccu-
pied with his thoughts, as though he were alone in the
office. "Barney Grant was standing at the end of the bar,
drunk as a skunk and grinning like a baboon, still holding his smoking Colt." Bert looked up as he lit his
cigarette. His face was taut.

Matt and Festus watched the silent ex-lawman. There was no question in their minds but that Bert Quinn had been deeply affected by what had happened in Pawnee that rainy night. Perhaps it had been the catalyst that had caused him to shift away from his previous life into a better one.

" 'You gonna lock me up?' Barney said." Bert looked at the two men watching him. "That's all he had to say after killing two fine men in cold blood. He was grinning when he said it. I think that was the straw that finally broke the camel's back."

"So?" asked Matt.

"He turned his back on me and reached for a whiskey bottle. Something snapped inside of me. Something that had been drawn wire-thin for months on end, maybe years, while I did Ned Grant's dirty work in Harker County and watched that drunken boy growing up, throwing his weight around Pawnee, knowing damned well that no one would dare interfere with him."

"But you did, eh, Bert?" asked Festus in anticipation.

Bert smiled a little thinly. "Yes," he replied. "I damned near bent the barrel of my Colt alongside his thick head and dropped him to the floor. I picked him up by his gun belt and dragged him from the Bella Union out onto Grant Street and through the mud and manure to the *calabozo* where I heaved him into a cell."

Matt smiled. "I never would have believed you had it in you."

Festus slapped his thighs. "By Godfrey! I wish I'da been there to see that sight!"

"I'm surprised you're still alive," said Matt.

Bert waved a hand. "I won't tell you how I got out of Pawnee alive that night. I was followed, I think, by one man, which seemed strange at the time, but I dropped his horse and got away from him. I twisted and turned, changed my guise and clothing, and think I might have thrown anyone off my trail while I was working my way here to Dodge City." He smiled a little thinly. "I've chased enough outlaws in my time as a lawman to learn some of their tricks and dodges, Matt."

"And why did you come to Dodge?" asked Matt.

Bert looked at his cigarette as though he had never seen one quite like it before. "For two reasons, Matt. First, I need a job. I'm dead broke, but I wouldn't take any of the money I had back in Pawnee because of the way I had earned it. I want no part of it now. Second, I don't know of any place in Kansas, perhaps in the West, where I'd be safer from Ned Grant and his *corrida* than right here in Dodge, at least while you're marshal here, Matt."

"Thanks," said Matt quietly.

Bert waved his hand.

Matt leaned back in his chair. "You're putting a great deal of responsibility on me."

Bert shook his head, "No," he corrected Matt. "I don't expect you to be my bodyguard while I'm here in Dodge, Matt. What is more important is the fact that Ned Grant may know better than to send any of his *corrida* here to Dodge looking for me as long as you're marshal here."

"Quite a compliment."

"But true," said Bert.

"Amen," said Festus.

Matt stood up and reached for his hat. "Be that as it may," he said. "I think I might be able to get you a job, if you want one."

"That's fine of you, Matt."

"Ever tend bar?" asked Matt.

Bert shrugged. " 'Bout twelve years back."

"Are you willing to try it again?"

"I haven't got much choice."

Matt shook his head. "I don't want you to take this job I might be able to get for you if you think that way, Bill."

"You misunderstood me, Matt. I'll take any kind of honest job I can get and do my damnedest to make a go of it," said Bert.

Matt nodded. "Can't ask for any more than that. So happens that Miss Kitty, owner of the Long Branch, needs an additional bartender. I'm going to take you over there to meet her and recommend that she give you the job."

Festus shrugged as he looked past Bert toward Matt. He wasn't too sure that Matt was doing the right thing.

Bert drained his coffee cup and buttoned his coat. "Are you planning to tell her who I really am?"

Matt nodded. "It would be better if she knew," he replied.

"Can we hold it there then? I wouldn't want it to get around town. You know how word gets around in this country. First thing you know, someone would pass the word along to Ned Grant and that would be the end of me."

Matt nodded again. "She'll be the only one who'll know about it outside of Festus and myself. I'll also tell my deputy Newly when he comes in. I'm sure he and Festus will keep their mouths shut." Here Matt gave the cold eye to Festus, who turned uncomfortably away.

"Yuh can bet on me, Bill Simpson," said Festus over his shoulder, "no matter what *some* people around here think."

Matt and Bert walked out into the street. Bert put on his blue-tinted glasses. "Maybe I'm only fooling myself with these things," he said, "but I think they help."

Matt smiled. "You fooled me for a little while with them." He walked toward the Long Branch. "You're still taking a terrible risk," he added. "You're sure you want to go through with this? If you want to, I can loan you enough money to get you out of the state to about any place you might want to go."

Bert shook his head. "I can't keep on running," he said quietly. "I've got to make a stand somewhere. If Ned Grant sends his paid killers after me I'll make my stand right here in Dodge." He walked silently for a little while and then looked sideways at Matt. "Have you come to the stage in life where you know you can't ever go back?"

Matt nodded.

They walked together through the windy darkness toward the lights of the Long Branch Saloon.

Chapter 5

Hank Johnson hadn't learned of Bert Quinn's hasty exit from Pawnee until early morning on the day after the escape. He had wandered casually into the sheriff's office to see if Bert Quinn would recognize him, only to find Anson Crowder swearing in Lem Martin as the new sheriff of Harker County. Hank wasted no time in setting out after Bert Quinn. No one in Pawnee seemed to know in which direction Quinn had gone. He had simply galloped into the rainy night; the next day he was as vanished as the rain.

The only clue to Quinn's route of escape came from Banjo Bates, the night operator of the telegraph office, who claimed that he had seen a burly horseman riding a blocky gray heading east and north on the road that led after quite a few empty miles to the Saline River Crossing. It wasn't much to go on, but Hank had nothing else in mind, so he followed the road toward the Saline River Crossing, hoping that the Four Horsemen or others of Ned Grant's *corrida* had not beaten him in the pursuit of Bert Quinn.

Hank rode his dun hard all that day and far into the night knowing that he must sacrifice the horse in order to make up the time he had lost while Quinn was making good his escape.

All night long Hank relentlessly forced the dun on

and on, feeling the horse's stride falter and breathing become erratic, knowing that the horse would never be any good after that night.

In the faint gray light before dawn Hank looked down the sloping ground toward the distant line of willows and cottonwoods that marked the course of the Saline River. The road trenched to the left to follow the course of the river until it reached the crossing. Hank reined in the exhausted dun and studied the line of trees through a battered pair of fieldglasses. Nothing moved. There was no sign of smoke.

Hank swung down from the saddle and led the dun on, studying the rain-soft ground for signs. He was tired, hungry and thirsty, but he would not stop to rest, eat or drink. His hatred of Bert Quinn drove him on relentlessly.

It was close to nine o'clock in the morning when Hank found trace—a line of deep-set hoofprints heading toward the river and the line of trees that marked its winding course. He studied the line of trees through his field-glasses. Nothing moved. There was no smoke.

Hank mounted the dun and urged it on following the line of hoofmarks. A rifle went off in the breaks and the fitful morning wind carried the rolling echo across the river south beyond the breaks. The dun was flung sideways by the impact of the bullet and went down. Hank kicked his right foot out of the stirrup and rolled sideways out of the saddle, ripping loose his Winchester '73 from the saddle scabbard. He levered a round of .44/40 into the chamber and snapped a slug toward the drifting gunsmoke.

Hank reloaded the rifle and peered toward the trees. The unseen rifleman fired again and this time the slug whispered evilly right past Hank's head. He jumped over the horse and hit the dirt behind the dead animal, softly cursing himself for his stupidity in standing in the open like a cornfield scarecrow. He thrust his rifle across the saddle and fired at the gunsmoke almost at the same instant. He raised his head and saw a burly man running through the trees and out of sight. A moment later he picked up the dull sound of hoofs thudding on the soft riverbank earth.

Hank ran forward with ready rifle, risking another shot, and plunged into the trees. He went from tree to tree like a turkey hunter and looked across the wide brown flood of the Saline River. A heavy-set man sat a blocky gray horse on the high ground beyond the far riverbank, then turned his horse on the forehand and galloped it north and east until both horse and rider were out of sight.

Hank leaned his rifle against a tree. He had no way of knowing that the rifleman had actually been Bert Quinn. True, the man had the burly figure of the ex-sheriff and he had been riding a blocky gray, but that didn't conclusively prove that it *was* Bert Quinn. Hank looked around.

A dying fire covered with a thick fur of ashes was in a hollow. Now and then the cat's-paw wind would stir the ashes and a secretive red eye would peep out and as quickly vanish, as though surreptitiously watching Hank. The sunlight glinted from a cracked mirror placed in a tree crotch. A battered enamelware coffeepot stood in the embers and a tin pan half-full of beans stood to one side.

Hank walked back to his dun and managed to get the saddle off. He carried the saddle back to the hollow and sat on it while he finished off the beans and coffee. He shaped and lighted another cigarette and then began to go over the hollow with a fine-tooth comb hoping to find some means of identifying the man. Closer to the river-bank he found a place where the man had evidently squat-ted on his bootheels and shaved himself. Hank turned over the scuffed-up earth and found traces of shaving soap mixed with salt-and-pepper hair of the type Bert Quinn had in his mustache. He walked back to the camp and examined the ground around the tree where the mirror was placed in a crotch. He found traces of brown dye on the trampled earth. Yet none of this proved that the man who shaved was Bert Quinn.

Hank kicked out the fire. He looked about himself and saw a dark, flat rock amid a pile of others that were lighter colored. He knew that the underside of a rock was always darker than the topside due to its contact with the earth. He turned it over. In a dug-out hollow he found a pair of gray trousers and a dark coat and crumpled gray hat. He nodded. They were articles of clothing that Bert Quinn had worn the night Hank had seen him in action in the Bella Union.

Hank cached his saddle and took his Winchester. He waded into the shallow waters of the Saline and worked his way across through chest-deep waters until he reached the far bank. He cast about until he found the fresh hoofmarks on a softer patch of ground and set out to follow them. By noon he had lost them and found himself on a narrow rutted road that seemed to come from nowhere to head into nothing.

He plodded along the road with the hot sun beating down on him. About half past five in the afternoon he saw a hawk circling slowly over the bosque of cottonwoods that spread across the road ahead of him. He moved on cautiously with his rifle at the ready and full-cocked. The hawk veered off on the wind and hung high over the bosque like a scrap of charred paper against the clear blue sky.

Hank moved silently through the trees. He looked out on the road where the rain had evidently puddled, forming a deep layer of soft mud. A big gray horse lay there in the middle of the road with its right front leg thrust out at an awkward angle and with a blackish bullet hole behind its right ear. It had no saddle. Hank was quite sure it was the same gray he had seen that morning. He followed the deep boot tracks sunk into the soft road. The man was evidently carrying the saddle and his rifle, the extra weight driving his heels down deep with every long-legged stride.

It was dark when Hank saw the lights of a ranch house far across the emptiness of the fields. He plodded on, softly cursing his luck.

The rancher was in the barn mending some harness when he had the eerie feeling that someone was watching him from behind. He turned slowly and saw a tired-looking man standing tall in the doorway with a Winchester held in the crook of his left arm. The man smiled. He turned over the left side of his coat and revealed a badge pinned to his shirt. It was too far for the rancher to see what it had printed on it. He slowly stood up. "Can I help you?" he asked.

"The name is Henderson. Sage Henderson," said Hank. He had bought the badge in a hock shop in Topeka not long after he had been finally freed from the state pen and had set out on the vengeance trail. "Lost my horse this morning. Shot out from under me on the other side of the Saline. I've been walking ever since. The man I'm following is a burly type. About fifty years old. Gray hair that is probably dyed brown. No mustache, freshly shaved off. Wearing light coat and trousers, dark hat. Scar hardly noticeable high on left cheek. About your height." He was careful not to mention Quinn's name. Quinn would likely be fairly well known even this far from Pawnee.

The rancher nodded. "There was a man looking like that here about supper time. He said he had to kill his horse about five miles back because it broke its leg. Had supper with us. Nice fella. Bought a nice claybank from me and left right after we ate."

"He say where he was going?"

"Toward the Solomon River country."

"That's a lot of country, mister."

The rancher shrugged. "That's all he said."

"Did he give you a name?"

The rancher shook his head. "And I didn't ask him. I know better when I see a man moving that fast through Kansas."

Hank nodded. "I'll need a horse," he said.

"Haven't got another one for sale."

Hank looked about. There were four workhorses and a riding horse in stalls. "What about that light bay there?" he asked.

"Not for sale, mister."

The Winchester was slowly leveled. "I'm on state business, mister. That bay is for sale, *isn't* he?"

The rancher looked down at the black muzzle of the rifle and then up into the cold gray eyes of the lawman. He nodded.

"I'll need a saddle, too."

The rancher saddled the bay. He led it out of the stable. Hank handed him the money for the horse. "That enough?" he asked. The rancher shrugged. Hank rapidly emptied the Winchester's magazine and handed the rifle to the rancher. He kneed the bay and set off at a gallop toward the road.

Late in the afternoon of the day after he had seen Bert Quinn, or whom he was quite sure *was* Bert Quinn, Hank Johnson realized he'd never find Bert Quinn with his method. The country was much too big, too empty, too sparsely inhabited. No one had seen a man answering to Hank Johnson's description of Bert Quinn, riding a claybank. Then, perhaps, he might have changed horses again, dyed his hair another color, put on a false mustache, and vanished into limbo.

Hank stayed that night in Pascoe and in the morning sold the light bay and took the afternoon train east to Topeka, on the long, long shot that Bert Quinn might be heading east. It was all he had to go on.

Chapter 6

Hank worked for two weeks in Topeka, rebuilding his dwindled grubstake in order to continue his relentless pursuit of the elusive Bert Quinn. He questioned anyone and everyone he met and always the same way: "A burly man, say about five feet ten inches or so, weight maybe one hundred and ninety. About fifty years old. Gray hair probably dyed brown or black. Clean-shaven. Very faint scar on upper left cheek." The answer was always the same: "Nope, haven't seen anyone like that, mister."

One night when Hank was on his way to bed he stopped in a saloon near the railroad station and got into conversation with a general storekeeper's clerk up from Walnut Creek to do a little buying for the store. "Yeah," he said thoughtfully. "I recall such a man. A little more than two weeks ago, though. Came into the store and bought a secondhand suit, a Kansas City hat and a pair of blue-tinted glasses. His eyes looked pretty good to me, but of course, you can't tell them things off-hand."

"Do you know where he went?" asked Hank.

The clerk shrugged. "Who knows? They come and they go."

"Was he riding a horse when he left town?"

"Hell! I don't even know if he *had* a horse. 'Bout the time he left town, though, the early afternoon train was just leaving for Topeka here. He might'a been on it. Well, anyways, as I was saying . . ." His voice died away. He

60

looked about. The man with whom he had been talking was gone, leaving only the swinging batwings to mark his fast exit.

The westbound night train was whistling for a crossing as it slowed down to pass through Topeka on its long trip hauling a string of freight cars behind it. As it passed the central street of the town a tall, lean man swung expertly aboard one of the flat cars.

Hank Johnson dropped off the westbound freight as it moved slowly through Walnut Creek. He headed for the livery stable at once. A man was seated on a chair slanted back against the wall chewing tobacco and expertly hitting a spittoon placed on the far side of the room while he flipped cards into a hat placed on the floor. He looked up as Hank came into the stable. "He'p you?" he asked.

"I'll likely need a horse," said Hank.

"What you mean, 'likely'? You either do or you don't," said the liveryman.

"Depends on the answers to some questions I want to ask you."

"I ain't no information booth."

Hank turned over the left-hand side of his coat and revealed his hock shop badge. "I'm looking for a man. Burly, about five feet ten inches or so. Gray hair probably dyed brown or black. About fifty years old. Clean-shaven. Very faint scar on upper left cheek."

The liveryman wrinkled his brow. He looked down at the five-dollar bill held out in Hank's hand. He nodded. "He came in here a coupla weeks ago. I traded off a good sorrel horse for his claybank and fifty bucks to boot. The claybank was about foundered. He must have ridden the hell out of it. The man looked pretty foundered, too, like he'd been riding all night, and was maybe afraid to stop."

"Which way did he go after he left here?" asked Hank.

"I ain't sure, mister."

Hank held up another five.

"South, I think. Yeah, a farmer comin' into town told me he had seen the man riding fast to the south."

"What's the nearest fair-sized town to the south?"

"Larned."

Hank Johnson bought a small gray and a beat-up saddle. He rode into town and bought a battered secondhand Winchester. When he left Walnut Creek heading south on the Larned road, he had exactly fifty cents in his pocket, a box of dry crackers and a can of sardines.

"There was a man here in Larned a few weeks past," said the liveryman in Larned to Hank Johnson after Hank flashed the badge on him. "Nice fella. Lightnin' rod salesman. Said his name was Bill Simpson and selling was his game. Kansas City man he said he was. Nice fella."

"Yeah," said the plump waitress in the Busy Bee Restaurant as Hank Johnson laid down his last fifty cents for stew and coffee. "I remember him. 'Bill Simpson is the name and selling is my game.' Always laughing. Wasn't so old I would'a taken to him myself."

"Which way did he go?" asked Hank.

She shrugged her plump shoulders. "Once they walk out that front door, mister, and they ain't regulars from town here, I never bother to watch which way they go."

"Bought a pair of overalls, a huck coat and a straw hat," recollected a storekeeper, the third one Hank had asked. "Didn't figure him for being a farmer but his money was good."

"Which way did he go?"

"East, I think. Yeah, it *was* east. I walked outside after he did to get my lunch and saw him riding east."

"What's east?"

The man grinned. "About half of the great State of Kansas, mister."

"I mean, any towns?"

The storekeeper shook his head. "Not much until you

reach the other side of the Great Bend of the Arkansas. Hutchinson is your best bet. Nice place. I got a cousin runs a secondhand clothing store there. Name of Peters. Look him up if you need some secondhand clothing."

"Do you say that to all of your customers?" asked Hank thoughtfully.

The storekeeper nodded. "Sure do, and my cousin always tells traveling people about my place. Good advertising and it don't cost a red cent."

"Thanks!" called back Hank as he ran for the door and his horse.

Hank rode across the empty, dusty sixty miles of the Great Bend of the Arkansas and reached Hutchinson the next day.

"Never saw anyone like you describe," said Sam Peters.

"You're sure?"

Sam nodded. "How's Jim?" he asked.

"Jim?"

"My cousin in Larned."

"Oh, fine!" Hank walked out into the bright sunshine. It took him two days of questioning until he found a hock shop where the owner showed him a .50/95 Express Winchester he said had been hocked by a man answering Quinn's description. Hank remembered all too well the heavy slumping sound of the big-bored rifle as it had gone off to kill his horse and also whip past his head. Quinn could have easily killed him. Why had he not done so? It had puzzled Hank ever since it had happened.

"Try Wichita," suggested the ticket seller in the railroad station. "Boom town, Wichita. Good place for a man to find work. That's what I tell all you drifters."

Hank sold his horse and boarded the train for Wichita, carrying his saddle and his rifle.

He was flat broke when he reached Wichita. He had to let the trail cool even more than he had wanted to in order to get some cash. He worked as a dishwasher during the days and as a saloon swamper nights for about two weeks, still asking his questions about the elusive Bert Quinn. Once again he had run up a blind alleyway and he was getting discouraged.

On a bright fall day he walked to the railroad station and stood on the platform looking first to the east and then to the west, trying to decide, if he had been in Quinn's shoes, which way *he* would have gone. "East," he said at last. "Somewhere out of Kansas."

Hank turned to go back inside and then slowly turned around as he heard two men talking on the platform. "Dodge City is the place for work now," said one of the men. "I'm selling out my store here and heading for Dodge myself. The place is booming. Railroad work. Cattle drives end there. Plenty of different kinds of businesses. Construction. Any man willing to work can find a job there."

The other man shrugged. "I've thought of it," he said. He looked at the other man. "You've been talking up Dodge City to everyone that ever came into your store."

The storekeeper laughed. "So I have. So I have. See you later, Ben." He turned to go.

"Mister!" called out Hank. He showed his badge. "Do you recall ever giving that advice to a man about fifty?" He held up a hand to show about five feet ten inches of height. "Weight about one hundred and ninety pounds. Gray hair maybe dyed darker. Faint scar on upper left cheek. Might be using the name of Bill Simpson."

The man nodded. "Came into my place some weeks past asking for clerical work. Didn't look like no clerk to me. I advised him to go to Dodge City."

"Did he go?"

The man shrugged. "Beats me. Why don't you go to Dodge and find out?" He walked away from Hank.

Hank walked inside the station. The ticketseller looked up sleepily. "I'm looking for a man," said Hank. "Fifty

Latest U.S. Government
tests of all cigarettes
show True is
lower in both
tar and nicotine
than 98% of all other
cigarettes sold.

Think about it.
Shouldn't your next cigarette be True?

Regular: 12 mg. "tar", 0.7 mg. nicotine,
Menthol: 12 mg. "tar", 0.8 mg. nicotine, av. per cigarette, FTC Report Feb. '73.

Latest U.S. Government tests of all menthol cigarettes show True is lower in both tar and nicotine than 98% of all other menthols sold.

Think about it.
Shouldn't your next cigarette be True?

© Lorillard 1973

so. Burly. Heavy man. About my height. Dyed hair. aint scar on left upper cheek. Name of Bill Simpson."

A swamper was mopping out the station. He looked up uickly as Hank questioned the ticketseller.

"Look, mister," said the ticketseller wearily, "I sell undreds of tickets a month. Most of the time I don't ven look up to see who's buying them. I can't help you."

"Mister?" said the swamper.

Hank turned. "Yes?" he asked.

"There was a man in here maybe a month or so ago ho looked like the man you're looking for. Looked like lawman. Fact is, he *was* a law man."

"How do you know that?"

"I recognized him but he didn't recognize me. I useta now him some years back."

"Where?"

"Pawnee, up in Harker County."

Hank came closer to the swamper. He held out a five-ollar bill. "Keep talking," he said quietly.

"Name wasn't Bill Simpson, though. It was Bert Quinn. ell you the truth, I got the hell out'a here as fast as I ould make it! I thought he might be lookin' for me. uess he wasn't. Maybe he was on a manhunt like they ay in the dime novels—incog—"

"Nito," finished Hank. "Where was he heading?"

"Dodge City, mister."

Hank handed him the five. He could hear the west-ound train whistling for a crossing east of town. He ought a ticket for Dodge and walked out onto the plat-rm. When the train arrived he carried his saddle and fle aboard and stowed them, dropped into a seat, stuck is ticket in his hatband and promptly dropped off to eep.

Hank Johnson got off the train in Dodge City. He

lugged his rifle and saddle onto Front Street and looked up and down the busy thoroughfare. He was going broke again. If he didn't locate Bert Quinn in Dodge City he'd be forced to go to work long enough to build up a substantial grubstake. If he did find Bert Quinn and killed him, he'd have to go on the run again and he'd need money to finance a speedy escape. Either way he had to find a job.

Carrying his gear, he trudged down the street to the Long Branch Saloon. He walked inside and placed the saddle at his feet and leaned the rifle at the end of the bar.

"What's your pleasure?" asked Sam, the head bartender.

"Beer," said Hank. He shoved back his hat and placed a foot on the brass rail, eyeing the fine free lunch close to his elbow. "Busy place," he observed.

"Always is," said Sam. He placed the beer in front of Hank.

"Any good games going?" asked Hank. He smiled. It was a foolish question to ask in Dodge City.

"Always are, mister." Sam mopped the bar. "You're new here?"

Hank nodded. "Just got into town from the east. Heading west when I get a grubstake."

"Plenty of work here. Railroad. Businesses. Cattle. What's your line?"

"Buffalo hunting."

"About petered out, ain't it?"

Hank nodded. "That's why I'm looking for work."

"Well, if you want to get a grubstake the fast way there are plenty of games going on. I hope you're good at it. We've still got plenty of cardsharps around in Dodge."

"Crooked deals?"

Sam shook his head. "Not too many. A crooked gambler doesn't last too long around here, especially not in the Long Branch. Miss Kitty, the owner, won't allow it

d besides, Matt Dillon is marshal here. You've heard
him?"

Hank nodded as he sipped his beer. "Who hasn't?"
: asked. He would not ask Sam about a burly man,
tyish, weight of about one hundred and ninety pounds,
/e feet ten inches tall, with dyed hair, faint scar on
per left cheek, maybe wearing blue-tinted glasses and
ing by the assumed name of Bill Simpson.

Sam busied himself along the long bar. Hank leaned
1 an elbow and fashioned a huge sandwich from the free
nch and munched at it as he looked at the men seated
the tables, hunting for 'Bill Simpson'. Maybe Bert
uinn had changed his disguise, but he could hardly
aange that burly shape of his no matter how hard he
ied.

A man came out of the back room tying an apron
out his waist. "All right, Sam," he said. "Time for
ur relief."

"Thanks," said Sam as he walked toward the end of the
ar and ducked under it.

The relief bartender came along the bar eyeing the
inks to see who needed refilling. He stopped behind
ank Johnson. "You ready for a refill on that beer, mis-
r?" he asked pleasantly.

For a stunned second or two Hank Johnson was frozen
to position. His mouth was full of meat and bread
ut he could not chew. Slowly, very slowly he low-
red the sandwich and just as slowly turned to the right
look into a broad face, the face of a man with dyed
air, wearing blue-tinted spectacles, with a very faint scar
n his upper left cheek. He was about five feet and ten
ches tall and probably weighed about one hundred and
inety pounds. The man was clean-shaven, although he
could have affected a shaggy dragoon-type mustache.

"The name is Simpson," said Bert Quinn. "Bill Simp-
on. Simpson's the name; bartending's the game. Been

working these past weeks as relief bartender. I know a
the regulars by now. You're new here, aren't you? A
least to me." He held out a big hand.

"Just passing through," said Hank. He gripped th
proffered hand. "The name is Carson. Henry Carson.
Carson was his mother's maiden name.

The hard gray eyes of Bert Quinn studied Hank closel
through the blue-tinted glasses. "How do they call you?
he asked.

"Hank is good enough."

Quinn nodded. "They usually do when your first nam
is Henry. I haven't been called William since I left hom
years ago. Always Bill."

"I'll bet you haven't," agreed Hank a little drily.

"What's your line of work?"

"Buffalo hunter. Retired now, I guess." Hank shrugged
"The buffalo have been about wiped out. All cattle coun
try out there now and that isn't my line of work."

"You're looking for work?"

"I have to. Used up my last grubstake. Moving wes
again as soon as I get some more money. I haven't ever
got a place to stay in Dodge."

"So? Too bad." Bert tilted his head to one side
"Haven't I seen you somewhere before?"

Hank shrugged. "It's possible."

"I hunted buffalo for a time in the early days whei
the hunting was good. Can't recollect seeing you ou
there."

"The Plains are mighty big," said Hank.

"I wonder though," mused Bert. "I could almost swea
I had seen you somewhere before."

"Can't imagine where." Hank felt for the makings an
took them out, busying himself with a cigarette to avoi
that damned penetrating gaze of Bert Quinn's. Most law
men had a fantastic memory file of wanted men. Still, i
had been ten long years since Bert Quinn had sav-

gely beaten a younger Hank Johnson and had had him
ent up on a rigged charge. Hank had aged a great deal
more than ten years while he had been in the State Pen.

"You a Kansas man?" asked Bert suddenly.

"Born in Missouri. Raised in Ioway. Worked in North
Kansas these past years."

"That makes you a Kansas man, then."

Hank lighted his cigarette and looked over the flare of
the lucifer into the hard gray eyes of Bert Quinn. "Guess
t does," he said around the cigarette. He dropped the
match into the spittoon. "Guess I'll move on," he added.

"If you're broke, friend, I can stake you to more beer,"
offered Bert.

Hank shook his head. "I like to pay my own way."

"Look," said Bert quickly. "I've got a big double room
over at Bascom's Boarding House. Two beds. Hell, I can
only sleep in one at a time." He laughed. "Go leave your
things there and stay with me a couple of days anyway,
until you get settled. I know how it is walking into a
strange town, busted, with no place to sleep."

"I can bunk down in the livery stable until I find work."

Bert shook his head. "No friend of mine has to do
that."

Hank looked steadily at Bert. Was the exlawman
putting on an act? Did he really know who Hank was?
Was he setting up a trap for the man who had sworn
for ten years to kill him? Hank was a good judge of men.
He had learned well in his ten years of prison. Bert Quinn
seemed sincere. What better chance would Hank have to
exact revenge on Bert Quinn than by establishing himself
as a friend? It was a good gamble.

"What do you say?" asked Bert.

"You've made a deal," said Hank. He held out a strong
hand and gripped the strong hand of Bert Quinn.

"Bascom's is two streets down and one over. You can't
miss it," explained Bert. "Another thing, Hank: I'm

hardly ever there. I've been working long hours here
learning the business, relieving the other bartenders, helping out wherever I can. You won't see much of me over
there."

Hank nodded. "Well, unless I find work, I won't be
around very much anyway."

"Speaking of work, did you ever tend bar?"

"I have," replied Hank. "I'm pretty green at it, but I
think I can make out."

"Maybe I can talk to Miss Kitty about you. We could
use another man." Bert grinned. "Fact is, if I can find
a relief man to replace me, I can get on as a regular. So
you see, I've got a motive."

Hank smiled. "There always has to be a motive for
about anything a person does."

Bert nodded. "What do you say?"

"Suits me, Bill."

Hank walked over and got his saddle and rifle. He
walked to the door and pushed his way through the
batwings.

Bert Quinn washed the beer glass, but his eyes were on
Hank Johnson through the window glass until the man
passed out of sight. Bert dried the glass and then walked
down to the far end of the bar to serve a customer. Now
and again, as he worked that day, he would mentally
finger through his memory trying to come up with someone who fitted the description of a lean, hard-looking
man, aged before his time, who might just fit the description of Henry "Hank" Carson.

Chapter 7

The farm had been abandoned for over five years. It hadn't been much in the first place, and the passage of the years and the neglecting of it had advanced its ruin. The house sagged in the middle and the barn sagged at the ends. The windmill hung at an angle like the Tower of Pisa and the rusting wheel turned slowly in the fitful night wind. Ranks of dusty weeds had grown along the sides of the house and the dilapidated barn. The buildings were set back from a rutted, single-track road that threaded its way through a bosque of cottonwoods to eventually meet the road that five miles away crossed the wide Arkansas River into Dodge City. Not a light showed anywhere in the area. It was poor farmland and the grazing was worse, so there were no other farms within five or six miles.

"Take a look around the place, Kid," ordered Mark Manton. The five men stood at their horses' heads in another bosque adjacent to the Dodge City road, looking toward the abandoned farm. It was four days before the planned raid on the Dodge City Bank.

The Kid stooped and unbuckled his roweled spurs. He unsheathed his Winchester '73 and padded off into the darkness as silently as a hunting cat. The dry wind rustled uneasily through the bosque and across the open fields.

"Who's gonna be there, anyways?" asked Barney.

"Looks like there ain't been anyone around here in about ten years."

"Five, to be almost exact," said Mark Manton. "There probably isn't anyone around there, Barney, but we're taking no chances."

The five of them had ridden away separately from Pawnee at one-day intervals and had worked their way toward the Dodge City area by different routes. Barney traveled with Mark Manton, for two reasons: none of the men trusted him alone and they weren't sure that he wouldn't end up in some saloon shooting off his loose mouth about the raid.

"Waste of time," grumbled Barney.

Sid Kellar looked at him. "I don't know about you, sonny," he said quietly, "but I ain't putting *my* neck into a noose by getting careless at this stage of the game. This is damned dangerous country for people like us."

Barney laughed. "My God!" he sneered. "Five hard-cases like us and you four act like scairt old ladies when a mouse runs across the floor! What is it you're *really* afraid of? Is it Matt Dillon? He ain't even gonna be there!"

"We can't be sure of that," said Sid.

Monk Cole leaned against his horse. "I'd like to try that *hombre* some time," he said thoughtfully.

"Hear! Hear!" cried Barney.

Monk looked quickly at Barney. "That ain't to say I wouldn't be damned careful how I went about it. Sid is right, though. We ain't come all the way down here to Dodge City just for any of us to try the big man. We came down here to get our fingers into a couple of hundred thousand dollars."

"Hell," said Barney. "Instead of all this damned hiding out in the woods and all these fancy plans we ought'a ride right into town in broad daylight like the James

Boys done and hit the bank, then shoot our way out'a town. Let 'em all know who we are! Ned Grant's Boys!"

Monk Cole rolled his eyes upwards. "Listen to him," he said.

Barney felt for his tobacco pouch and took it out of a shirt pocket. He began to shape a cigarette.

"What the hell do you think you're doing?" demanded Mark.

"Gonna make a smoke," replied Barney. "Is there a law against that, too?"

Mark snatched the makings out of Barney's hands. "Hell yes! A light can be seen for miles out here!"

"Who's to see it?" demanded Barney.

Mark hurled the tobacco into the brush.

"Goddamn you!" snapped Barney, "You got no right to do that!" He dropped his hand to his Colt. That was a mistake. He found himself staring fixedly at a razor-edged knife blade held in front of his face. "You dumb sonofabitch!" warned Sid Kellar. "You pull any more stupid tricks and I'll cut your throat from ear to ear!"

Monk growled in his throat. "Send the runt back," he said. "Get rid of him! He'll get us all killed!"

Mark put a hand on Sid's knife wrist. He shook his head. "It's too late," he warned. He walked to the edge of the bosque and looked toward the farm. Only the possibility that he might need Barney later as a hostage against Ned Grant had led him to interfere with Sid's knife play.

A soft whistle sounded through the darkness. The Kid came silently through the bosque. "All clear, Mark," he reported. He looked closely at Mark. "What's the matter?" he asked.

Mark pulled away from the group and jerked his head backwards. "It's Barney," he said.

"You don't have to tell me," said the Kid. "Do we have to take him along?"

Mark nodded. "There's no way out of it now."

The Kid rubbed his lean jaw. "You know," he said quietly, "once we get the loot we can always get rid of him." He grinned. "You know what I mean, a wild shot in the back. Who's to know who did it?"

Mark shook his head. "No. Not until we're in the clear. Then we can get rid of him."

"Allow me," said the Kid with a smile.

Mark laughed drily. "You're liable to have to wait in line."

They walked together back to the others.

"Take off your spurs," Mark ordered.

"The windmill still works," said the Kid. "There's fresh water in the tank. There's even some feed left in the barn. Some of the furniture is still in the house."

"The Kid will go ahead," ordered Mark. "The rest of you follow him at five minute intervals. Put your horses in the barn and water them there."

"Waste of time," grumbled Barney.

The Kid led off, followed by the others one by one, with Mark bringing up the rear leading two extra horses. They led the horses into the barn and closed the big door behind themselves.

"We'll bunk in here, men," said Mark. "It'll be less conspicuous. We'll cook our grub burning dry wood during daylight hours. There will always be one man with the horses. The rest of us can stay in the house during the day. One man will always be on sentry duty outside."

"Sounds like a damned military campaign," said Barney.

"It is," said Mark.

"That's why we've always made out," added Sid. He looked sideways at Barney. "That's why we're going to make out this time, too."

"Why are you tellin' *me?*" demanded Barney.

Sid turned away in disgust.

Mark Manton lighted a bull's-eye lantern and turned the shade so that the light could not be seen from the outside. "Starting tonight, each one of us will go in turn into Dodge to familiarize himself with the layout of the town, the site of the marshal's office and the bank, the routes to and out of town for when we make the raid. There will be no drinking." He looked quickly sideways at Barney. "The Kid will go into town first and will stay there until early Sunday morning, making sure Dillon is out of town, and that the situation will be all right for the raid."

"Why him?" asked Barney. "I can handle that end of the job."

Mark ignored him. "When you go into town, Sid, check the bridge for the spot where you'll plant your explosives the night we go in on the raid. You'll have to plant them in the dark, so know exactly where you want to place them."

"Why not do it now?" asked Barney brightly. "Then we don't have to waste the time doing it when we raid the bank."

The Kid looked slowly at him. "You can't mean that," he said.

"Why not?" demanded Barney.

"Because some nosy bastard may find them!" snapped the Kid. "You ever think of that?"

Barney shrugged. "I was only trying to help," he said in an aggrieved tone.

"I want each of you to know the central part of the town as though you had been born there and had lived there all your lives," instructed Mark. "I want you to know the alternate routes of escape I've laid out: the interior of the bank; the alleyway in the rear of the bank. *Everything!* Nothing must be left to chance. Go over the routes in the daylight and at night. Any questions?"

Barney opened his mouth and then closed it.

"Good!" said Mark. "If anything looks suspicious, even the simplest thing, I want you to report it to me. Understand?"

They all nodded.

"Stay inconspicuous. Remember that you're not going in there to enjoy yourselves. You're going there to work! Once we get the loot and get to Mexico you can enjoy yourselves for the rest of your lives. But not now! Stay out of the saloons, gambling halls and whorehouses. Another thing: the Kid will leave tonight and stay there until Sunday morning, as I've already told you. If any of the rest of you see him in town, ignore him."

"That'll be easy," said Monk. He grinned.

"Monk, you're the best cook. We'll risk one fire tonight to prepare a hot meal, but make it fast."

"Beans, bacon and hard bread," said Monk. "It won't take long."

"Is that the best you can do?" grumbled Barney.

"You want to go hungry, sonny?" demanded Monk. "This ain't exactly Delmonico's in Dodge, you know."

One by one the men got water for the horses and watered them within the barn. Monk made a dry wood fire in the rusty kitchen stove, heated his beans and fried his bacon, then put out the fire and brought the food to the barn. No one spoke while they ate. The time was getting close for the big hit and each of them was occupied with his own thoughts.

The Kid led his buckskin horse from the rear of the barn and into the bosque, then led him to the main road where he mounted up and rode on into Dodge.

Chapter 8

The Laredo Kid took his buckskin to a livery stable and left him there. He'd been in Dodge a few years before while on his way north to join Ned Grant's *corrida*, but he hadn't been there long enough to really learn the town. He stood across the street and studied the bank, which was closed for the night. He walked further and found the site of the marshal's office as depicted on Mark Manton's precise chart of the town's street layout.

The Kid crossed the street to the marshal's office and walked inside.

Newly looked up from his newspaper. Festus was sound asleep in a chair tilted back against the wall. "Help you?" asked Newly.

"I wanted to see Marshal Matt Dillon," said the Kid with one of his most winning smiles. He was good at it.

"The marshal ain't in town," said Newly.

"That's too bad," said the Kid.

"What's your trouble?" asked Newly.

"Nothing. No trouble. I was just wondering how the deputy situation was around Dodge. Always had a hankering to be a deputy down my way. Texas, that is. Laredo. They tell me I haven't got enough experience. I said they should take me on to get some experience." He grinned. "Everyone wants you to have job experience but they ain't willing to give you a job to teach it to you."

"Ain't that the truth?" asked Festus, awakening.

"Well, I got to thinking who was the best lawman in the business," continued the Kid. "Matt Dillon, I says one day! He's the best. So, I got on my horse and rode all the way up here to Dodge to go to work for him."

"We got all the deppities we need," said Festus.

"Well, it was a good thought."

"You got any experience at all?" asked Newly.

The Kid shrugged. "I was on a posse once. In Texas, that is."

"Takes mor'n one posse to make a good lawman," said Festus. "Now, look at me. I—"

"I learn fast," interrupted the Kid.

"I'll just bet you do," said Festus. "How long you gonna be around town?"

The Kid shrugged. "Couple of days, I guess."

"Well, the marshal ain't due back until Monday. He got a hot tip that a wanted man was seen a couple of times around the Wichita area. He left this afternoon to go there."

"That a fact," remarked the Kid. "Well, I'll just hang around until Monday, then, to see the marshal personal-like, if you got no objections."

Newly shrugged. "Not me, young fella. How do they call you?"

"The name is Benson. Art Benson." That was his Uncle Art's name, the one who was strung up in Fort Worth for too much horse-stealing. The Kid could hardly remember him so it was hardly possible that these Kansas hicks would remember him, either.

"I'll tell him you called," said Newly.

The Kid walked to the door, turned and flashed one of his most charming smiles. *"Vaya,"* he said. He closed the door.

Newly got up and walked to the window. He watched the Kid cross the street. "Now, who the hell was that?" he asked over his shoulder.

"Nice-lookin' young feller," said Festus. "We sure could use someone like him around here. To meet the public-like."

Newly nodded. "Sure could, and it might put you out of a job, Festus."

"Who, *me*? Fat chance! The marshal couldn't get along without me. Why, I . . ."

Newly grinned. "Why don't you give him a chance to find out?" he slyly asked.

Festus opened and then closed his mouth. He walked to the window and peered through it. He could see the Kid standing across the street in front of the bank. "Seen a fella like him once before," he mused. "Young, say about twenty-one, fair-haired, blue-eyed, and always smiling, smiling all the time. Looked like he wouldn't hurt a fly."

"Yeah? Who was it?" asked Newly.

"Name of Bonney," said Festus. "William Bonney."

"Can't say that I've heard of him."

"He was better known as Billy the Kid," grinned Festus. He slapped his thighs and guffawed. "Caught yuh, Newly!"

The Laredo Kid drifted along the streets around the bank and the marshal's office in the central part of the town. He ducked into the alleyway behind the bank and checked it out, passing behind the Long Branch Saloon further down the alleyway. He came out at the next street intersection and wandered about like a Texas cow-poke just in from a cattle drive seeing the Big City, fabulous Dodge, for the first time.

Bert Quinn came out of his boarding house. He was due as relief on the night shift at the Long Branch. Sam wasn't feeling well, hadn't been feeling well for a couple of days, but he was stubborn and didn't want to quit work. He walked to the street and unlatched the gate. He felt for the makings as he walked toward the next street intersection. He shaped a smoke and then felt for his lucifers to find he had none. A slim young man was leaning casually against a street lamp with a cigarette dangling from the corner of his mouth.

"You got a light, son?" Quinn asked.

"Sure do, old timer," said the Laredo Kid. He thumb-snapped a lucifer into flame and held it to the tip of Bert's cigarette. Bert Quinn's guts seemed to congeal as he looked into the guileless blue eyes of the Kid. He drew back his head as he got the light. He coughed suddenly, removed the cigarette, and covered the lower part of his face with his left hand.

"Jesus, old timer," said the Kid sympathetically. "You'd better lay off the smokes. That's a bad hack you got there."

"Thanks for the light," gasped Quinn. "Got to get to work, son." He hurried off, coughing and gasping all the way until he turned the corner.

The Kid shrugged. "Crazy old coot," he said to himself.

Bert Quinn walked into the Long Branch, nodding to the customers and Hank Johnson who was being broken in behind the long bar by Sam. He walked into the rear store room and took off his coat, removing a double-barreled Derringer from one of the pockets to slip it inside a trouser pocket. He put on his apron as Sam came through the door. Sam looked closely at him. "You look like you seen a ghost."

Bert nodded. "Maybe I did, Sam. Maybe I did." He hurried out to get behind the bar under which was a sawed-off, double-barreled Greener, like the one he had used in Pawnee for emergencies. He made sure it was in position.

"You all right, Bill?" asked Hank.

"Sure, sure," said Quinn. He wiped the cold sweat from

his face. If the Laredo Kid was around, the rest of the Four Horsmen could not be far off.

A cold pre-dawn wind was sweeping the valley of the Arkansas when Sid Kellar dismounted at the end of the bridge across the river from Dodge City. He slowly led his dun across the bridge until he reached the middle of it. There was no one in sight. The town was still asleep. He ground-reined the dun and then let himself down over the side of the bridge and into the web of bridge supports about ten feet above the smoothly flowing river. He opened a bull's-eye lantern and quickly lighted it, closing the shutter and opening the lens cover to put a little spot of light on the joints of the supports. In a matter of minutes he had selected the places for his charges. Judiciously chosen, the selected spots would, if blown, take out the center section of the bridge for about twenty feet. He put out the lantern and clambered back up over the side of the bridge.

He led the dun into the railroad yards and into an open shed, laying down on a pile of shavings and going to sleep. The light of the sun streaming into the shed awoke him. He got up, walked the dun into town and tethered him outside of Delmonico's Restaurant. He bought a newspaper and went inside the restaurant to order breakfast before he made his inspection of Dodge.

Bert Quinn opened the Long Branch that morning. He liked the morning and early afternoon shifts the best. He was a little tired because of working late the night before and because seeing the Laredo Kid had caused him to lose most of the night's sleep.

"I'm going across the street to get breakfast, Benny," he told the swamper. "Take over until I get back."

Miss Kitty came down the stairs from her quarters.

"Bill!" she called out. "If you're going over to Del
monico's please bring me back my usual breakfast."

Bert Quinn smiled. "With the greatest of pleasure, Mis
Kitty," he said.

Quinn walked across the busy street into the restauran
and sat down at the long counter. He ordered breakfas
for himself and then looked into the back mirror behin
the counter, peering through his blue-tinted spectacles
trying to figure out if the Laredo Kid had really recog
nized him. Quinn couldn't tell. Granted he looked differ
ent, but he might only be fooling himself.

The waitress placed his order in front of him.

"I'll want Miss Kitty's breakfast," said Bert. "You ca
have it made while I'm eating."

"Something new?" the waitress asked. "Miss Kitty usu
ally has her breakfast with Marshal Dillon."

"The marshal is out of town," said Bert Quinn.

A man reading a newspaper in one the booths sud
denly looked up toward Bert Quinn. Quinn bent his heac
over his food. He peered up into the rear mirror of th
counter. "My God," he muttered to himself. He was look
ing right into the reflected saturnine face of Sid Kellar

Kellar looked down again at his newspaper. Bert Quinn
ate quickly, picked up the dish containing Miss Kitty'
breakfast, paid for both meals and hurriedly left the res
taurant. He took the breakfast to Miss Kitty in her office

Kitty looked up as he entered. "What's been troublin
you, Bill?" she asked.

"Nothing, Miss Kitty. Why? Hasn't my work been al
right?"

"Fine," she said. "just fine. But I noticed you were
nervous last night. You kept looking at the doorway and
at the clock as though you couldn't wait to get out of
here."

He smiled. "Just a little tired is all, Miss Kitty. You
know I've been working extra shifts since Sam hasn't

been feeling well, besides helping break in Hank Carson.
Oh, I'm not complaining. I'd rather be working than not
working."

She nodded. "I feel the same way." She watched him
curiously as he left the office.

Hank Johnson was polishing the glasses as Bert Quinn
came out of Miss Kitty's office. "You all right, Bill?" he
asked.

"Fine. What are you doing here?"

"Miss Kitty said you seemed tired last night. She
asked me to come in this morning and give you a hand.
I hope you don't think I'm trying to take over your job,
old friend."

Bert shook his head.

"You were damned restless last night," said Hank.

Bert shrugged. "Something I ate, I guess."

Hank watched Bert work along the bar serving the
early morning customers. Something *was* bothering the
man. Hank figured on keeping a close eye on him.
Maybe he was wise to Hank by now. Hank would have
to watch his every step.

Monk Cole rode across the Arkansas River bridge
Thursday evening on his way into Dodge for *his* inspection tour. He passed Sid on the bridge but neither of them
gave a sign of recognition to the other.

Monk tethered his claybank a block from the bank
and the marshal's office. He sauntered about the streets
with a long-nine cigar sticking out of the side of his mouth
like a river steamer's jackstaff. He had never been in
Dodge before but he had no difficulty recognizing the
street layout and the sites of the bank and marshal's
office from the chart Mark Manton had made. For a
time he stood at his post where he could cover the front
of the bank and the marshal's office at the same time,

checking ranges up and down the street for the use of his long gun in case of sudden trouble. It should be a cinch. He could keep any citizens or lawmen under cover and then duck into the alleyway behind the bank to follow Sid and Mark as they led the horses out to the next street, giving them covering fire as he did so to hold off any pursuit through the alleyway.

He sauntered into the alleyway as though to relieve himself and then checked the rear of the bank. Sid should have no trouble with *that* door. Monk thought he might be able to rip it off his hinges with his bare hands. He grinned at the thought. "Save blasting powder and noise," he said in a low voice to himself.

Bert Quinn was on the night shift again, working with Hank Johnson. Hank was working in well. He was quiet, but efficient, and learned quickly. Bert looked at Hank. "It's quiet right now," he said. "I'm going to change that empty keg."

"I can do it," offered Hank.

Bert shook his head. "Tend the bar, friend," he said. He disconnected the empty beer keg and rolled it from behind the bar. He rolled it into the rear storeroom and then unlocked the alley door to put the empty out on the rack behind the saloon. The yellow lamplight from the storeroom formed a lean rectangular pattern on the rutted mud of the alleyway.

Quinn rolled the keg to the rear doorway and bent to pick it up to carry it to the storage rack outside the saloon.

"Want a hand with that, friend?" asked Monk Cole from just behind Bert.

Cold sweat broke out on Bert as he recognized the voice of Ned Grant's strongarm killer.

"Kinda heavy, ain't it?" asked Monk.

"It's empty," said Bert Quinn, trying to change his voice.

Together they lifted the heavy keg into the rack, Bert making sure he stayed out of the light of the opened doorway. "I owe you a drink or two, friend," he said.

"No," said Monk. "Not tonight, anyways."

"Come in any time," offered Quinn as he walked into the storeroom, keeping his broad back toward Monk.

"Sure will," said Monk. "Not for a while, though." He laughed at his private joke.

Bert kept his head bent low as he started to close the door. "Who do I look for?" he asked.

"The name is Smith. Joe Smith."

"I'll remember," said Bert. He closed the door and shot the latch. Cold sweat broke out on his face and body. By God! Then there were three of the Four Horsemen in Dodge City—The Laredo Kid, Sid Kellar and Monk Cole. That left Mark Manton, the most dangerous one of the bunch, dangerous because he could think. Maybe Bert had fooled the first three of the Four Horsemen but he had no illusions about fooling Mark Manton. There was only one reason they would be in Dodge—to find and kill Bert Quinn.

Bert's first impulse was to shuck his apron and get to hell out of Dodge City—*fast!* Then he shook his head. The brave words he had spoken to Matt Dillon the night he had arrived in Dodge City came back to him: *"I can't keep on running. I've got to make a stand somewhere. If Ned Grant sends his paid killers after me I'll make my stand right here in Dodge . . ."*

Bert rolled a full keg of lager beer through the doorway of the saloon and then behind the bar.

Hank Johnson looked curiously at him. "What took you so long, Bill?"

"Lost my way," said Bert Quinn drily.

Hank grinned. He had a nice grin. "Figures," he said.

Together they placed the keg and connected it. Hank eyed the other man curiously. "You all right?"

"Stop asking me that!" Bert snapped testily.

"Easy," cautioned Hank. "I was just trying to help."

"Sorry," said Quinn. He looked around the crowded barroom as though expecting to see the Four Horsemen walk in through the batwings and come gunning for him. It wasn't likely. That was not their way. Not in Matt Dillon's Dodge, in any case. The shot in the dark; the knife in the back; the bullet unseen from the dry gulch. That was the way of Ned Grant's *corrida*. Bert Quinn should know.

Hank came along the bar to serve a customer. "You're doing O.K.," Quinn said.

Hank shrugged. "Bartenders are just ordinary people. The only difference between them and ordinary people is that somewhere in life a bartender had his brains knocked out, but he never knew it."

Bert Quinn grinned. Hank was all right. "That's the experience you've had," he said. Hank grinned back at him.

Chapter 9

The Laredo Kid was looking for Barney Grant. Barney had taken his turn Friday night in coming to Dodge City. Instead of studying the layout of the town and the area around the bank, he had made what the army usually called a cursory inspection and then had headed for the nearest bar and after that a sleazy bawdy house down near the railroad yards. He had lasted twenty minutes in there. The madam, alerted by the screaming of one of her younger girls, had had Barney, cursing and fighting, heaved out into the street. Barney still had enough sense left to keep his engraved Colt in its sheath, but he didn't have enough sense not to head for the Long Branch Saloon.

The Kid had seen Barney from a distance earlier in the evening, but he had wisely kept out of the way. He had ridden quickly out to the farm and had notified Mark Manton, who cursed a savage streak and ordered Monk and Sid to go to the bridge and wait for the Kid to deliver Barney to them. He, himself, would not go. "I'd be afraid I might kill the drunken sonofabitch," he had said bitterly. "We can't afford that."

The Laredo Kid had immediately returned to Dodge to track down Barney, hoping to find him in a dark alleyway where he could knock him out and bring him across the river where Sid and Monk would pick him up. He'd almost regret not being able to see the dressing-down Mark Manton would give Barney. He grinned at the thought.

The Laredo Kid had no luck in trapping Barney in an alleyway. He finally trailed him through a few other saloons, all of which had ejected him, into the Long Branch. When the Kid came quietly into the crowded room he saw Barney at the end of the long bar, holding onto it with one hand while he swayed back and forth waving the other hand and talking to one of the bartenders at the top of his voice.

Hank Johnson knew that Barney didn't know him or of him. He quietly listened to Barney and his drunken drivel. He wondered of course why the young fool happened to be in Dodge. Bert Quinn, the man who, not a month or so past, had buffaloed the big-mouthed Barney into unconsciousness and had dragged him through the mud and manure of Grant Street to heave him into a cell, kept his distance, working the far end of the bar. Quinn wanted no part of Barney Grant and he was getting help. Hank tried to keep the two men as far apart as possible too. He wanted Bert Quinn for himself.

Bert Quinn, behind his blue-tinted spectacles, now and again slid his eyes sideways to watch Barney Grant. He knew now they were after him. But why send Barney? He could not be trusted out of sight of anyone in authority over him, although there was really only one man who held any authority over Barney, and that was a rather nebulous thing, for he seemingly did not want to or could not exert any control over him. That one man was Ned Grant.

And where was Mark Manton? That was a greater puzzle to Bert than the presence of three of the Four Horsemen and Barney Grant in Dodge. He was the truly deadly one—the man behind the scenes, the manipulator of his less intelligent henchmen.

Bert served his drinks and polished the drinking glasses,

the while hearing Barney's loud, rattling voice coming to him above the usual barroom noises—the humming of conversation, the clicking of the roulette wheel, the clacking sound of the chuck-a-luck cage being whirled about, the clinking of glasses.

Barney suddenly realized he wasn't getting much attention. He wasn't used to that. He still hadn't learned the difference between notoriety and popularity. "Drinks for the house!" he roared.

Hank made his decision. He wanted Bert for himself. Any minute now Barney might recognize Bert Quinn and that would mean a sudden shoot-out. "You've had enough, mister," Hank said quietly. He rested his hand on the bung starter mallet that was kept under the bar.

Barney stared incredulously at him. "You know who I am, bartender?" he asked.

Hank shook his head. "Can't say that I do."

"If you did, you'd serve me like I told you to."

Hank shook his head again. "Happens I don't. It's a house rule not to serve drinks to anyone as drunk as you are."

"You saying I'm drunk?"

Hank smiled. "Well, aren't you?"

"Who's the owner here?" demanded Barney.

Everyone could smell the trouble emanating from the young man. They were all watching him.

"Miss Kitty is the owner," said Hank.

Barney simpered. "A woman! Miss Kitty Cat!"

"Someone go get Marshal Dillon," said Doc Adams who was seated at a rear table.

"He's out of town," a man said.

Barney heard them. He turned. "Good for him," he said. "I been wanting a showdown with that hardcase."

A man rapped lightly on Miss Kitty's office door. She opened it and the man pointed to Barney. "Trouble," he said in a low voice.

Hank leaned forward, shifting his hand for a better grip on the bung starter. "Look, mister," he said evenly. "We don't want any trouble with you. Now please leave."

The Laredo Kid hovered in the background. This was a touchy situation. He had to get Barney out of there but he knew he'd never be able to do it quietly. It would be just like the loudmouth to shoot off his mouth about the proposed hit, or at least give some evidence of it away. The Kid rested his hand on his Colt. He might have to kill Barney to keep his mouth shut, but he'd have to make it look legal. That is, if Barney made a break for his own Colt.

Kitty came across the room and stopped behind Barney Grant. "What's the trouble?" she asked.

"This *gentleman* has had too much to drink, Miss Kitty," Hank explained. "I've refused him service, but he refuses to leave."

Barney turned slowly. He looked Miss Kitty up and down. "Jeeeesusss," he said. "Where the hell they been keepin' you, sister?"

"He's done it now," murmured Doc.

Barney turned and slapped a hand down on the bar. "Booze," he said. "For me and the lady here."

"No," said Hank.

"Goddamn you!" roared Barney. He slapped his hand down for his always-ready Colt. The Laredo Kid moved in, shifting about for a clear shot at Barney. Barney's Colt came up swiftly. Even with a lot of booze in him, he was very good with his gun. His thumb dragged back on the big spur hammer, letting the weight of the Colt cock itself.

A full quart bottle sailed through the air, past Hank Johnson's upraised bung starter. The thick bottom rim of the heavy bottle caught Barney edgewise on the left temple. He staggered backward. The Colt exploded sending a blast of flame and smoke toward Hank Johnson.

The .44/40 slug skinned past Hank's head and through his thick hair. He winced at the burning sensation of it. The Laredo Kid ran forward and caught Barney as he fell.

"I hope the sonofabitch is dead," said a customer. "Begging your pardon, Miss Kitty."

The Laredo Kid looked up from where he knelt on the floor beside Barney. "I know who he is," he said. "His old man is a friend of mine down Texas way. Help me get him out of here."

"He nearly killed a man tonight," said Miss Kitty.

"I'm all right," said Hank. "I'll have a headache tonight, that's all, Miss Kitty."

"You've got a hard head, Hank," said Bert Quinn.

"He should be held for charges," said Doc. He knelt beside Barney and looked at him. "He'll be all right," he said to the Kid. "He just got a good buffaloing, is all." He smiled. "First time I've ever seen such a fast draw with a bottle, Bill. I'd like to see you handle a sixgun like that."

Hank looked sideways at Quinn. The man could still go into deadly action and accuracy with any weapon at hand. It wouldn't be easy to kill him.

Doc leaned over and looked at Hank's head. "Damndest thing I ever saw," he murmured. "Looks like a pencil line on that hard skull of yours, Hank."

Hank smiled. "I'll live," he said. "Often felt my thick skull would come in useful some day."

"He was just passing through," offered the Kid. "I'll get him out of here and he won't be back again. I can promise you that." He looked up at Hank. "You want to prefer charges?" he asked.

Hank shook his head. "Get him out of here and don't let him come back."

"I'll see that he leaves Dodge," said the Kid.

Barney opened his eyes. "Whiskey," he groaned.

The Kid helped Barney to his feet. He holstered Barney's Colt for him and helped him to the batwings. They pushed through to the street.

"Let's get to drinking again, men!" Quinn called out cheerfully.

"On the house!" cried Miss Kitty.

Hank came over to Bert when the serving of drinks had temporarily slowed down. "*Gracias,* partner," he said quietly.

Bert casually waved a big hand. "*Por nada,*" he countered.

Hank shook his head. "It was not for nothing," he corrected.

"It was, to *me.*" Bert looked sideways at Hank. "I wouldn't want to lose the best friend I've got in Dodge City," he said. He means it, thought Hank.

"You would have done the same thing for me, wouldn't you, Hank?" asked Bert.

Hank nodded. He wanted to save Bert Quinn for that final showdown some day.

Bert looked up at the big wall clock. "Can you take over for a few minutes?" he asked. "I've got an errand to do. It won't take me long."

Hank nodded. He watched Bert strip off his apron and round the bar to leave through the batwings. He shrugged.

Bert Quinn half-cocked his Derringer as he walked down the busy street. He wasn't yet sure that he had not been recognized. He hurried along until he saw the Laredo Kid leading a horse with Barney sagging in the saddle toward the plank bridge over the Arkansas. He ducked behind a riverbank shed and watched the Kid lead the horse to the far side of the wide river. In a little while the Kid came back, walking fast, to disappear into the dark sidestreets of Dodge.

Bert hurried to the telegraph office and entered it. He snatched up a message blank and hastily scrawled a message: "Three of Ned Grant's Four Horsemen here in Dodge area, with Barney Grant. No sign of Mark Manton. They may, or may not be after me. Can't tell yet. Something in the wind? Best return at once." He signed it "Bill Simpson" and handed it to the night clerk. "Send that marked Urgent to Marshal Matt Dillon, c/o Marshal's Office, Wichita, Kansas," he said.

The clerk nodded. "Right away."

"When will he get it?"

"It will be there in half an hour. That's not to say, though, that Marshal Dillon will get it that fast. He might not be in town."

"You'd better pray that he is," said Bert. He leaned closer. "This is confidential." He placed a five-dollar bill atop the message. "Can I leave by the back way?"

The clerk shrugged. "Help yourself, mister."

Bert hurried back to the Long Branch. He doffed his coat and put on his apron, then ducked behind the bar to join Hank Johnson.

"Anyone ever tell you that you were a good hand with a whiskey bottle?" Hank asked him.

Quinn grinned. "How do you mean that?"

They laughed heartily together.

Chapter 10

The westbound Santa Fe freight train slowed down for the Dodge City freight yards late Saturday night. Matt Dillon dropped off the caboose and waved goodbye to the freight conductor. He passed between the cars standing on a siding and catfooted through dark alleyways until he reached the rear door of the marshal's office. He tapped on the door.

Newly walked quickly to the rear door of the office. "Who is it?" he asked.

"Matt Dillon," replied Matt. "Is there anyone else in there?"

"I'm alone, Matt."

"Any prisoners?"

"None."

"Open up then. Go and lock the front door and then draw the shades as soon as you unlock this door."

Newly unlocked the door and then walked to the front of the office to draw the shades and lock up.

Matt slipped inside and locked the rear door behind him.

Newly came back to Matt. "What are you doing back in Dodge this late at night?" he asked.

"Is there coffee?"

"Plenty."

Matt helped himself to a cup and warmed himself by the stove. "Where's Festus?"

"Over at the Long Branch keeping an eye on things."

"What's up over there?"

Newly quickly told Matt about what had happened the night before when Barney had gone loco in the saloon.

"Did you know that three of Ned Grant's Four Horsemen have been in Dodge since I left?"

Newly shook his head.

"Bert Quinn didn't tell you?"

"No."

Someone tried the front door and then shook it. "Doggone it, Newly!" cried Festus. "What you got this door locked for, anyways? It's cold out here!"

"Open up, Newly," instructed Matt.

Festus came in. His jaw dropped when he saw Matt. "What are you doing back here, Matthew?" he asked.

"Bert Quinn sent me a telegram late last night, evidently after that ruckus in the Long Branch. He says that three of Ned Grant's Four Horsemen are in or around Dodge."

"Lordy!" said Festus. "And Barney Grant, too! We know the Laredo Kid was in there last night, because Bert Quinn told us this morning that it was him. Got a lot of nerve, that Kid. He come in here a couple of days ago all smiles and shiny white teeth and said he wanted to get taken on as a deputy because you were the best in the business, he said. Called hisself Art Benson!"

Matt shrugged. "Art Benson? The name rings a bell." He narrowed his eyes for a moment and then nodded. "Art Benson. Strung up about ten years ago by a vigilante committee in Fort Worth who got tired of him stealing horses. They say he was a past-master of the art. The Kid happens to be his nephew."

"How'd you remember that?" asked Festus.

"It's all part of the job that goes with the badge."

Newly grinned. "That'll take care of you, Festus."

"Well, anyways, the Kid said he'd be back Monday when you was supposed to come back, Matthew."

"Took guts to come in here like that," said Newly.

Matt nodded. "He was probably just keeping tabs on me. I think that call to Wichita was a ruse to draw me away from Dodge."

"But why?" asked Festus. "Because Grant's *corrida* is planning to kill Bert Quinn?"

Matt took off his coat and sat down at his desk. "I wonder?" he mused. "Quinn mentioned there was no sign of Mark Manton, and he's the most dangerous of the lot. He's the brains."

"All to the good, then," said Newly.

Matt shook his head. "No, there's something suspicious there. Another thing: why would Barney Grant suddenly show up in Dodge? I'll bet he wouldn't be welcome among the Four Horseman. I certainly wouldn't want that knuckleheaded drunk working with me on anything as dangerous as trying to kill Bert Quinn, especially in Dodge."

"Because of you," said Newly.

Matt waved a big hand.

"Barney and the Kid probably didn't recognize Bert Quinn," said Newly. "At least they didn't act like it."

"The Kid would be too smart for that," said Matt.

"Bert told me that he saw the Kid taking Barney across the bridge that night after the ruckus," said Newly. "The Kid came back alone. It's a cinch there must have been someone on the other side of the bridge waiting for him."

"Sid Kellar and Monk Cole, most likely," put in Festus. "I been keeping an eye out all day for them. The only one of the bunch I've seen is the Kid."

"It's loco," said Newly.

"The only reason for them being here we have to go on," mused Matt, "is that they came over to get Quinn.

They most likely haven't recognized him, at least Barney and the Kid haven't."

"Why would they go to all the bother of getting Quinn? He ain't doing nothing to them. All he wants is to be left alone." asked Newly.

Matt looked at him. "Simple enough. Bert knows too much about Ned Grant's operations and Grant also works on the idea that once you're a Grant man, you're *always* a Grant man. There's no way out of his organization except by death—by being murdered. *Executed* would be the better term."

"I find that hard to believe."

"You don't know Ned Grant, Newly. He's set himself up as a god in Harker County. Personally, I think he's a little crazy."

"So what do we do now?" Festus asked.

Matt drained his coffee cup and got up to refill it. "The two of you sit tight and run the office just as though I was still in Wichita. Festus, tomorrow you stay out in the streets and keep an eye on the Kid, and any of other of Grant's men who show up. Newly, before dawn you ride out across the bridge, don't let anyone see you, and scout around out in that area. For God's sake, be careful not to be seen! You'll be up against some of the worst hardcases in the state, so stay low watch your step! Now, tonight Festus will go over to the Long Branch and tell Kitty I'm back in town. I want to talk with her and Bert Quinn but I don't want anyone else in Dodge to know I'm back from Wichita."

"Wouldn't it be better to take Bert into protective custody?" asked Newly.

Matt shook his head. "Not unless he wants me to. Once we let him go, they'd likely be after him again. This way, we can use him as bait, although I don't like the sound of the word."

"Supposin' he don't like being bait?" asked Festus.

"Knowing Bert as I do," replied Matt, "he'll want a showdown on this deal. He can't live out the rest of his life knowing that any hour, or any day, they might want to settle their score with him. I wouldn't want to live that way and neither would you."

Festus left by the rear door and headed for the Long Branch. In a few minutes he came back. "All right, Matt," he said. "Miss Kitty and Bert Quinn will be waiting in the storeroom. There are only a few of the regulars in the place and it's almost closing time. Go in by the rear door."

Matt nodded. "You'd best come with me, Festus."

The two of them left the office through the back and walked quietly through the darkened alleyways. Festus tapped three times on the Long Branch's rear door and then three times again. Bert Quinn opened the door slightly and they both slipped inside.

"Thank God you're here, Matt," said Kitty.

Matt smiled. "Glad to be here," he said. "I think now that me going to Wichita was a ruse of Ned Grant's to get me out of town."

Bert nodded. "That's the way he operates." He took off his spectacles and rubbed his eyes. "What do you want me to do, Matt?"

"Sit tight, if you can stand the strain."

Kitty placed a slim hand at her throat. "Wouldn't it be better to either lock him up until they're gone, or get him secretly out of town?"

Matt shook his head. "They've come here to kill him. It's not their way to kill a man in the open in a fair fight. They're not likely to shoot him down on the streets of Dodge or here in the Long Branch just like that. They're not known in Dodge, at least until Barney made a show out of himself, and they likely mean to keep it that way. Their way is the shot in the dark or the knife in the back and no trace of who did it."

"Unless they don't want to kill him here, or kill him at all," suggested Kitty.

Bert looked quickly at her. "I never thought of that," he said. "I got too concerned about myself. After all, we don't really know if they recognized me. Barney certainly didn't. The way *he* was he'd hardly have recognized his own mother." He grinned. "Come to think of it, that wouldn't be too easy for him, either."

"It's a risk we'll have to take," said Matt. "I'll keep out of sight within the next few days. Festus and Newly are going to check around to see if they're still in the area."

"Does Hank Carson know about all this?" asked Festus.

Bert shook his head.

"Who's Hank?" asked Matt.

"Hank Carson," replied Bert. "Nice fella. Drifted into town like I did, dead broke and with no place to stay. I took to the man. He's bunking with me until he can get ahead, and works here in the Long Branch as bartender, learning the business like I am."

"Where is he now?" asked Matt.

"Behind the bar, getting ready to close."

Matt walked to the door and eased it open. He saw Hank washing down the bar. "What do you know about him?" he asked.

Bert shrugged. "Missouri-born. Raised in Iowa. Ex-buffalo hunter."

"That's all?"

"About all," said Quinn, "except I like him and I think he likes me."

"You never saw him before?"

"No."

"Not in Pawnee?"

Bert shook his head. "Why?"

"You ever figure that he might be one of Grant's *corrida?*"

"If he was, I'd know him."

Matt shook his head. "That's just it. If he's one of Grant's men and you don't know him, he'd be the most likely member of the *corrida* to be sent after you."

"Then why would the others be here?" asked Kitty.

Matt nodded. "A good point."

Kitty looked at Quinn. "Then you won't leave Dodge, Bert?" she asked quietly.

He shook his head. "I said I was through running. If they've come after me, I want the showdown *now*. I don't want to live on the run the rest of my life full of fear that every stranger I see might just be one of Grant's *corrida* hunting me down. Besides, I like it here. I've got a job I like and a boss I like. I've got some real friends here for the first time in my life. There's nothing out there beyond Dodge, Miss Kitty, besides loneliness and fear. I'd rather be dead than have to live like that."

Matt nodded. "I agree," he said. "We'll sit tight and see what happens."

Matt and Festus left by the rear door. Miss Kitty and Bert walked back into the barroom. The place was now empty of customers. Hank looked up curiously as they came back into the room.

Bert Quinn walked behind the bar as Kitty went into her office.

"Everything all right?" asked Hank.

"Couldn't be better," replied Bert cheerily.

They closed the Long Branch together.

Chapter 11

Barney Grant lay on a pile of moldy straw in the barn of the abandoned homestead. His head ached, not so much from the lump on it where the whiskey bottle had struck it as from the hangover he was suffering. His belly was uneasy and his throat was sour dry. He had a bottle in one of his saddlebags but he hadn't dared try to get it to ease his pounding head with some of the hair of the vicious dog that had bitten him. It was 1:30 Sunday morning and the Laredo Kid was due at the farm at almost any time.

"Two cards," said Monk Cole. He held up two fingers to Mark Manton. He glanced toward the rear of the barn where Barney suffered in silence. "I still think we ought'a finish that job the bartender started in Dodge," he said in a low voice. He looked at his Winchester. "One good hit with the butt of that '73 there and we'd be rid of that stupid, drunken sonofabitch back there. Of all the . . ." His voice died away in disgust.

"Shut up!" snapped Mark Manton. He dealt Monk two cards. "We'll have to wait until we pull this job. We can't risk sending him back to Pawnee. Besides, I want him for a possible hostage against his old man."

"It's a helluva risk taking him with us into Dodge," said Monk.

"It's a worse risk leaving him here." Mark dealt himself a card. "God knows what he'd do then."

Lightning crackled over the countryside followed by the rumbling sound of the thunder drums.

Sid Kellar came inside the barn. "We're going to have some dirty weather," he said adding, "there are hoofbeats on the road."

Mark wet his thumb and forefinger tips. He pinched out the candle flame. The three men moved like a well-oiled team. Monk picked up his rifle and walked out the rear entrance of the barn to take his position in a clump of rank weeds where he could cover the front of the barn and the road leading into the farm building area. Sid Kellar eased through the partly opened front door and took his position on the other side of the barn. Mark stood just inside the barn door peering through the opening.

"Who is it?" called out Barney.

"Shut up!" snapped Mark.

"I was only asking," said Barney in an aggrieved tone. "It's gotta be the Kid, ain't it?"

"We don't know that," said Mark.

The lone horseman drew rein at the Texas gate beyond the farmhouse and whistled softly three times and then three times again. Staghorn lightning flashed eerily across the sky lighting up the deserted countryside in a ghastly glow. Thunder thudded through the heavens. The Kid dismounted and led his buckskin through the Texas gate and toward the barn.

"Hi, Sid," said the Kid with a winning grin. "You pruning something in them weeds?" He led his buckskin into the barn as Mark slid the door open for him. Sid came into the barn closing the door behind himself. Monk came in through the rear door. Lightning flashed and thunder rumbled loudly over the farm like an ominous warning of what lay ahead.

"It's going to rain," said the Kid. "All the better cover for us. Ain't none of the good citizens of Dodge goin' to poke their noses out'a a warm bed on a cold, rainy Sunday morning at three o'clock."

Mark lighted the candle. "How's it look?" he asked the Laredo Kid.

The Kid shaped a cigarette and lighted it from the candle. "Perfect," he replied around the cigarette. "The town is asleep. Dillon is still in Wichita."

"Who's acting as marshal?"

"Deputy named Newly and that clown they call Festus."

"Where's Bill Gaines, the banker?"

The Kid shrugged. "Haven't seen hide nor hair of him. He's out'a town." He grinned. "Likely in Pawnee, talking business with Grant."

"You're sure he's out of town?"

The Kid nodded. "His house is across the alleyway just behind the bank. Guess he don't like to be too far from his dollars. Only ones in the house are his kid Billy, about ten years old, and a half-deaf old lady housekeeper. I went over to the house today asking if they had a room to let and the kid talks to me. Smart little whippersnapper. He wouldn't tell me where his old man was."

They all lit up. Barney Grant came shambling to the group and sat down on the floor with his back against a post while he rolled a cigarette. Mark took out the chart and spread it out on top of the box he and Monk had been using for a card table.

"Oh, my God," murmured Barney. He rolled his bleary eyes upwards. "We goin' through all that crap again?"

Mark looked sideways at Barney. "You want to pull out of this deal right now, mister," he said quietly, "you just say so."

Barney paused in lighting his cigarette. He looked from one to the other of the four pairs of hard, unblinking eyes staring at him. He slowly lowered the match.

"Well?" asked Mark.

I'd be dead in two minutes if I tried to pull out now, thought Barney. "I was only joshin'," he complained. "Can't you fellas take a joke?"

"Sure," Sid agreed, "but that was no joke."

Barney, far away from his doting father and the sheriff of Harker County, could not even find solace in a bottle. Now, partly sober, with a horrible hangover, he knew he'd never get out of this deal alive if he tried to quit. He'd have to stand on his own two feet for the first time in his useless, misbegotten life, just to keep these four hardcases from killing him.

Mark looked down at the map. "Kid?" he said.

"I go in first, cut the telegraph line. Scout the approaches to the bank and the marshal's office, come back and give the all-clear. Then I go ahead again and take position where I can cover my assigned area. When the hit is made, I stop any interference that might come along. I retreat on foot until a block from the bridge where you'll leave my horse, and Barney's and Monk's. Once you get across the bridge with the loot, Mark, I cross the bridge, passing Sid, who blows the bridge. Once on the other side of the bridge I head for the Cimarron country and later Texas."

"Monk?" asked Mark.

Monk leaned forward. "I go in after the Kid cuts the telegraph wire and scouts the town. I set up where I can cover the front of the bank and the front of the marshal's office. Once the hit is made I retreat with the Kid and Barney, covering you and Sid, until we reach our horses a block from the end of the bridge. I cross the bridge with the Kid and once on the other side I head for the Medicine Lodge country and then Texas."

"Barney?" said Mark.

Barney shambled over to the box and looked at the map. "I follow in after the Kid, along with Monk. I

cover the rear of the marshal's office and the rear of the
bank, from the street where I can see both alleyways.
When the hit is made I head for the bridge, helping cover
until I reach the horses. I cross the bridge and then head
west toward Colorado. Later I head for Texas."

Mark looked sideways at Sid.

"On the way in I plant my charges under the middle
of the bridge and lay the fuse. Once the Kid lets us know
the way is clear, me and you lead the horses in behind the
bank. You cover me while I blow off the rear bank door
hinges with squib charges. They won't be very loud, at
least not loud enough to carry to the marshal's office, if
there's anyone in there at that time of the night. The next
step is for you and me enter the bank. You keep watch
while I blow the vault door. We gather the loot, carry it
out the rear door, load it on one of the spare horses,
and we lead the horses to a block from the bridge where
we leave the horses for Monk, the Kid and Barney. You
ride on across the bridge with the loot. I stay behind to
blow the charges after the rest of you cross the bridge.
Once the bridge is blown, I ride south directly to the
Oklahoma line and straight to Texas."

"Good!" said Mark. "I go in with Sid and cover him
while he plants the bridge charges. We enter the town
after you three and take the horses to the rear of the
bank. I cover Sid while he blows off the rear bank door.
I cover him in the bank while he blows the vault. We
take the loot out to the horses and load it on an extra
horse. We lead the horses to a block from the bridge
and leave the three horses for you rearguard men. I
cross the bridge to the far side, dropping Sid off to blow
the charges after you three cross. I take the loot and head
east and then north toward the Buckner Creek country
where I cache the loot."

"Then what?" asked Barney.

Mark looked at him. "What do you mean?"

"Exactly *where* do you hide the loot?"

Mark looked at the others.

Monk nodded. "He's right," he said. "We all ought to know."

Sid nodded, too. "If anything happens to you, none of us will know where the loot is."

"Ned Grant will," said the Kid. He grinned.

"Wouldn't it be better if we divided up the loot and each of us took off to meet in Texas?" asked Sid.

"Just try it," said Barney. "My old man would track you straight into hell if you tried that, and you know he would."

Monk nodded. "Yeah," he agreed. "That's something to think about. He'd do it, too." He looked at Mark. "The Boss was always fair to me in any dealings. We gotta do the same now."

"I'll agree to that," said the Kid. "After all, it was him that thought up the whole deal and made the arrangements down in Coahuila. I couldn't have done it."

"Me neither," said Monk.

Sid shrugged.

"We can't change the plan now," said Mark. He drummed his long fingers on the chart. Only he and Ned Grant were to know where the loot was cached and for some time Mark had been seriously considering keeping the whole bag for himself and heading for Canada. But then there was always the threat of Ned Grant's revenge.

"Where?" asked Sid quietly.

Mark looked at him quickly. "What do you mean?"

"The hiding place," said Sid. "Where are we going to hide the loot after the bank job?" He spoke slowly and carefully.

"Hackberry Creek," replied Mark. "A place called Lone Bosque. A clump of trees that have overgrown a rocky knoll and with nothing but empty prairies on all sides. No one lives within fifteen miles of the place. In among the rocks there are all kinds of crevices. In one of the crevices is an old Indian grave. No Indian in his right mind would touch it because of the spirit there; no white man would touch it for fear of rousing up the Indians. It's a natural." He smiled. "Plus the fact that the place is infested with rattlers. Like insurance . . ."

Mark stood up and wound his watch. "It should take no more than twenty minutes from the time Sid and I reach the rear of the bank to do the job and be back on the bridge. Once that vault is blown every man in town will be up in arms. They'll come streaming into the streets heading for the bank. Barney, Monk and the Kid will be able to hold them up just long enough for me and Sid to reach the bridge. It will be close, but it's the best we can do."

"Listen," said the Kid.

Fat raindrops had begun to plop on the barn roof and on the hard, dry ground around the barn. A cool damp breeze blew through the cracks in the barn wall and through the gaps in the doorways.

"Let's move," said Mark.

Sid stowed his prepared powder charges in a tow sack. The Kid, Monk and Barney placed hide boots on the horse's feet, tying them about the fetlocks. Each man checked the magazine of his Winchester and the cylinder of his Colt. The horses were quickly saddled and led outside into the lightly falling rain.

Mark mounted his sorrel and took the reins of one of the extra horses. The led horse was a dun, a breed famed for bottom and staying power. He'd need it for his escape after he wore out the sorrel in his long flight cast and then north.

Sid slung his tow sack of explosives over the cantle of his saddle and mounted his horse. He had the reins of the extra led horse in his right hand. Monk, Barney and the Kid mounted their horses and looked at Mark. He punched his clenched fist out toward the road and touched his spurs to the flanks of the sorrel. Perhaps he was, in his own mind, remembering his days as a hell-for-leather rebel cavalryman serving under Fighting Joe Wheeler.

They rode along the dark, empty road through the rain with the staghorn lightning still flickering eerily high over head and the thunder grumbling away in the distance.

Mark drew rein at the approach to the bridge. Only a few faint lights shone mistily through the rain from Dodge across the wide Arkansas. The Laredo Kid, followed by Monk and Barney, trotted out on the bridge, their horses' booted hooves sounding hollowly on the planking. Mark and Sid followed them. Each man masked his face with his bandanna.

The Kid turned his buckskin and rode a little east. He drew rein beside a telegraph pole and stood up in his saddle to reach the high-set lineman's spikes set into the pole. He climbed to the crossarm and cut the wire and then held it in his hand as he returned to his horse. He wound the wire about his saddle horn and then galloped his horse along the road, stripping off about two hundred yards of wire. He cut the wire again and then dragged the loose wire down to the banks of the river. He quickly coiled it up and hurled it as far as he could into the dark waters. He rode back to Monk and the Kid. They tethered their horses to the bridge railing and then catfooted into the dark street with the Kid in the lead. The Kid passed on into the darkness and in a little while he came back. He nodded. He trotted back to the bridge, cupped his hands about his mouth and three times gave the mournful cry of a coyote. He returned to Monk and Barney and then went on to his post.

Monk and Barney worked their way up the alleyway toward the rear of the bank. They padded across a street intersection.

"You fellas got a drink?" a plaintive voice said out of a dark doorway.

Monk halted, head thrust forward. "Yeah," he said softly. "C'mere, friend."

The old drunk staggered out of the doorway. He smiled wanly in a lightning flash. "Jesus," he said. "This is like a miracle. I never had such luck before."

Monk's knife came up under the old drunk's rib cage and pierced his heart. Monk caught him as he fell. He carried him to a fence about an empty lot and dumped him over. "C'mon," he said to a somewhat shaken Barney.

Sid Kellar went agilely over the side of the bridge. Mark handed him the charges. Sid worked swiftly and efficiently planting the dynamite. He reeled out the fuse and fastened it under the railing top on the outward side.

They led the horses on into the darkened town and up the alleyways behind the bank. One of the two horses there whinnied suddenly. Mark clamped a hand on the culprit's nose. "Go ahead," he hissed.

In the second-floor rear bedroom of Banker Gaines' house whose rear faced the alleyway across from the bank young Billy Gaines had been awakened by the thunder and crackling lightning. He had distinctly heard the whinny of a horse from the alleyway behind the bank. He got out of bed and peered through an opened window toward the street.

Sid worked swiftly inserting his squib charges behind the big hinges of the bank's rear door. He attached the fuses and looked back at Mark. He nodded. Mark waved a hand. Sid lighted a lucifer and cupped it in his hands. He waited until lightning flashed and then touched off the fuse. The two minor explosions were perfectly timed with the crackling of the lightning and the subsequent thunder. The door sagged inward. Sid and Mark lifted it to one side. Mark went in first, Colt at the ready, and

scouted throughout the darkened bank. He whistled softly.
Sid came in carrying his tow sack. He set to work on the
vault door. It was an old timer, long past its prime. A
cinch. Sid smiled crookedly.

Billy Gaines padded softly down the rear stairway of
his house and stood in the rain with his head cocked to
one side. He was sure he had heard something explode,
mingled with the lightning crackle and the rumble of
thunder. He walked softly across the rear yard and
climbed over the fence to find himself looking at seven
horses standing ground-reined behind the bank. The rear
door of the bank lay to one side. Billy snuck quietly into
the old building.

Mark peered around the edge of one of the drawn
front window shades. He could see a man standing in the
doorway with Winchester ready in his hands.

Sid Kellar squatted back on his heels and began to un-
reel a length of fuse. Something made him turn his head.

Billy Gaines stood looking at him. "What do you think
you're doing here in my father's bank?" he asked.

Mark Manton clamped a hand over the boy's mouth
and was punished by having a fine set of sharp teeth
promptly sunk into his hand. "Jesus!" snapped Mark. He
swung out his Colt and tapped the kid on the back of his
head. He fell unconscious to the floor.

Festus was wide awake early that rainy Sunday morning. He had eaten a fine pork dinner at Delmonico's the
night before. It had been so fine in fact that he had eaten
a second helping. He was paying the price now. His belly
was bothering the hell out of him. He got up from his cot
and looked into the rear cell where Matt was sleeping
the sleep of the just and the guilt-free. Festus tip-toed
to the front door. He eased open the lock and turned

to look back at Matt. Newly was bunking in with Hank Johnson and Bert Quinn, keeping an eye on Bert until the Four Horsemen (less one) scare was over.

Sid Kellar looked at the softly cursing Mark who was sucking at his bitten left hand. He nodded. Mark cat-footed to the front of the bank. Sid lighted the fuse and ran from the vault to drop behind the high teller's counter. Mark hit the floor at the same time. The blast shattered the quiet and some of the disturbed air blew out the big front window of the bank shattering it and clattering it on the plank sidewalk outside. A gushing of thick, acrid smoke came from the vault and billowed through the building and out the broken front window. By sheer luck the blast had coincided with a particularly noisy crashing of thunder.

Festus yanked open the front door of the marshal's office in time to see the front window of the bank collapse and to hear the thudding of the explosion. He watched the pall of smoke that poured out into the street.

"Matt!" yelled Festus. "Somebody's just hit the bank! Now we know why the Four Horsemen were really here!"

A .44/40 slug fired from across the street struck the office door and drove a sharp sliver of wood into Festus' right cheek. He winced and slammed the door shut, dropping to the floor where he wormed his way over to the rifle rack as a second bullet shattered one of the front windows, struck one of the cell bars and richochetted.

Matt rolled from the bunk and snatched up a Winchester '73. "Keep that rifleman busy!" he yelled over his shoulder as he yanked open the rear door and slammed out into the alleyway. He jumped back behind a post and peered around it toward the street. On the far side of the street was the alleyway that led behind the bank. He could see the dim shapes of horses standing there by a faint lightning flash.

Matt ran down the alleyway. He saw a masked man peer around from a doorway looking toward the firing from the street intersection where Monk was pumping slugs toward the front of the marshal's office. The watching man held a rifle in his hands, obviously the lookout placed there to watch the rear of the bank and the rear of Matt's office.

Matt darted across the alleyway and rolled over a fence. He crawled along behind the fence and peered over the end of it to see that the lookout was still watching the other way. Matt crouched low, rifle training, and ran across the street, ducking into a doorway just as the lookout turned toward the mouth of the alley that passed the rear of the sheriff's office.

Matt waited until the lookout turned again and then he rounded the corner of the alleyway that led behind the bank. He yanked off his big hat and slapped the wet rumps of the horses. Lightning flashed right over the town. That was enough for the horses. The blast as the vault had been blown had already made them skittish. They galloped away at a fast clip.

Rain suddenly sluiced down as the lightning died in the dark heavens. Matt turned toward the bank. A masked man came running into the alleyway. "Damn you, Dillon!" he yelled. Lightning crackled and Matt saw the man's wet rifle barrel as it was raised. He dropped bellyflat in the mud, thrusting out his Winchester to fire just as a bullet hummed right where he had been standing. The man staggered backward gripping his left arm. He fell flat on his back. "I'm hit!" he screamed. "Don't shoot no more!" Barney Grant's fight was all out of him.

An unmasked man appeared suddenly in the doorway of the bank carrying what looked like a stuffed tow sack. He jumped to one side as he saw Matt and thrust out a pistol to fire. Matt rolled over and over and then up onto his feet, firing and levering his Winchester at hip level until the man fell heavily into the mud of the alleyway with his guts shot to ribbons. Sid Kellar had cashed in his chips.

Matt saw another masked man standing within the bank, holding a boy in front of him. Matt held his fire just in time. The masked man jumped back out of sight, firing toward Matt as he did so. The slug pocked a slat of the wooden fence just behind the marshal. He flattened himself against the rear wall of the bank.

"Don't shoot!" the man inside the bank yelled hoarsely. "I've got the banker's kid in here!"

Matt held his fire. Newly came running down the side street. "Get that wounded man out of there!" yelled Dillon.

Festus quickly slid a Winchester through a front broken window of the office and fired at the big man who stood uncertainly in the bank doorway. The slug slapped the man's rifle barrel and he threw it from his stinging hands. Someone in the bank opened the front door for him and he slipped quickly inside.

Down the street the Laredo Kid saw armed men running toward him. He looked the other way. Lightning flashed and he saw more men coming toward him. He sprinted across the street with slugs whining about him and dived through the shattered front window of the bank.

The firing died away. Lightning flashed and thunder rumbled and the rain slanted down through the drifting gunsmoke. Barney was screaming and crying like a child as Newly forced him into the marshal's office.

Doc Adams came at a run down the street with his medical bag in his hand.

"In here, Doc!" yelled Festus.

Matt saw Newly running through the alleyway. "Cover

the rear door," said Matt. "They've got a kid in there with them. Billy Gaines."

"My God," said Newly.

Matt nodded. He walked to the street and ran across it to the cover of a doorway. He could see men up and down the street peering out of houses and around corners, rifles and pistols at the ready.

Matt eased himself into the next doorway. "You there!" he yelled. "In the bank! You're surrounded! Throw down your guns and come out with your hands up!"

"Go to hell!" yelled Monk through the broken window.

More and more of the Dodge City armed citizenry began to show up. Bert Quinn and Hank Johnson came up behind Matt. "Now we know why they came here," said Bert Quinn.

Matt nodded.

"You want me to go and get them out?" asked Bert. He was willing enough to do it. It was always his way.

Matt shook his head. "They've got the banker's boy in there with them," he said quietly. He looked at Quinn. "Would they harm him?"

Bert nodded. "Don't take any chances, Matt. They are dangerous, desperate men."

"There are three of them in there," said Matt. "One of them is dead in the alleyway. Another one is in my office with a slug in his arm."

"Barney Grant," said Newly as he came up behind the group. "I've got three men watching the bank's rear door, Matt."

Dillon thrust out his head. "We've got your partner here!" he yelled. "Barney Grant! He's got a bullet in his arm. Will you trade for the boy?"

"Listen to *him!*" yelled the Kid. "That's the best joke of the night."

"The Laredo Kid," said Bert.

"Who else is in there then?" asked Matt. "Check the dead man behind the bank."

Bert walked quickly to the alleyway. In a quick flash of lightning he saw the rain-wet, contorted face of Sid Kellar staring up the streaming sky with eyes that did not see. Bert went back to Matt. "That's Sid Kellar back there.

"The two left are the Kid and Monk Cole," Quinn added.

"And the other one? The man who held the boy?"

"It must be Mark Manton. This job is like something he would have planned."

Matt nodded. "He might have gotten away with it, too, if Barney hadn't been out of position."

Doc Adams joined them. "Barney's got a broken arm," he reported. "He'll be all right."

"Too bad," said Bert.

"I passed Sam Gordon in the street on the way to your office," added Doc. "He's dead, Matt."

"So is Pat Meager," said a man standing nearby. "Rifle bullet through his head. It was the big fella that ran into the bank that done it."

"A bad night for Dodge," said another man.

"Dillon!" yelled the Kid through the half-open front door. His voice was muffled by his mask.

"What do you want?" called out Matt.

"Freedom to leave the bank and get a twenty-four hour start out of town."

"No!"

"You want to see the kid alive again, you'll agree."

"What're your terms?" shouted Matt.

"Let us out of here on your word of honor you won't shoot. We want our horses brought behind the bank. We want to cross the Arkansas and have a twenty-four hour start before you begin following us."

"Go ahead, Matt. You don't have to keep your word," urged Festus.

"What about the boy?" yelled Matt.

"We'll take him across the bridge with us and leave him on the other side."

"And the money?"

The Kid laughed. "You must be joking, Dillon!"

"We'll have to do it," muttered Matt.

Newly and some of the men rounded up the bandits' horses and brought them to the rear of the bank. They walked quickly to the street. In a moment the three men came out, stepping over Sid Kellar. The tow sack with the money crammed into it was tied over a saddle cantle. Billy Gaines was placed on a saddle and his legs tied under the belly of the horse. The three masked men worked swiftly. They mounted the horses and spurred them down the wet alleyway under the flashes of lightning and through the drizzling rain.

The Dodge citizenry ran through the streets after the fleeing outlaws. The horses thundered onto the bridge. Midway across one of the men slid his buckskin to a halt. He dropped from the saddle and thumb-snapped a lucifer into quick flame which he cupped in his hands.

Matt, Newly and some others ran out onto the bridge. The Kid held the flame to the end of the fuse and then swung up onto his horse. He turned and waved his hat. "*Vaya, amigos!*" he yelled. He bent low in the saddle and raced the buckskin toward the far shore of the river.

Matt stopped running. "Stay back!" he yelled.

Half a dozen men ran on.

Suddenly there was a blasting of flame and smoke from under the middle of the bridge. The center of it seemed to move up almost leisurely like an opening drawbridge and a gush of flame, smoke, sparks and bits of dark, shattered timbers sailed upward in a rapidly ascending column. Some of the running men were hurled

back by the blast as a piece of heavy timber fell. The
others ran back to Matt Dillon who stood white-faced,
watching the grisly scene.

The great rumbling echo of the explosion rolled along
the banks of the Arkansas and died away in the distance.
Pieces of debris splashed down into the dark waters, and
in a little while that, too, stopped. A great gap showed in
the middle of the bridge.

Lightning flashed. There was no sign of the fleeing
outlaws or of Billy Gaines on the far shore.

Matt Dillon turned quickly. "Jason," he told the
liveryman. "Saddle my gray and let me have another good
animal for a led horse. Newly, get a pair of horses and
come with me. Festus, get that telegraph line repaired
and get the operator moving. I want an alarm sent out to
every lawman in all directions for a hundred miles. I don't
want *one* of them left out! As soon as you're done with
that, organize a posse of the best men you can find and
follow our trail."

They all moved swiftly. Matt rammed his Winchester
into his saddle scabbard and mounted the gray. He took
the reins of a light bay and spurred the gray down toward
the dark waters of the river, followed by Newly riding one
horse and leading another. Matt splashed the big gray
into the water. It swam strongly, with Matt holding his
Winchester high over his head. Newly followed.

They struggled out onto the far shore and disappeared
into the rainy darkness.

"All right," said Festus. "Who wants to go along?"

Chapter 12

The rain stopped not long after Mark Manton, Monk Cole and the Laredo Kid, with Billy Gaines, had swum their horses back across the Arkansas ten miles east of Dodge City. A pale moon was trying to force its weak rays through the low overcast. Lightning flashed faintly far to the west and the distant sound of thunder rolled across the wet prairies. The hoofs of the horses splashed through puddles and patches of watery mud. Now and again one of the night riders would turn in his saddle and look back toward the south.

"We can take it easy," grumbled Monk. "Dillon gave us his word he'd not follow us for twenty-four hours."

Mark shook his head. "That was before the Kid blew the bridge up and likely killed and injured some of those people back there."

"Don't blame me," put in the Kid. "You were supposed to leave that boy back there instead of taking him along with us."

"He's life insurance," said Mark. "You know what would happen to us if we got caught? They wouldn't even bother with a trial. Those Dodge City hardcases would string us up without even offering a prayer." He looked back through the dimness. "Dillon is back there somewhere," he added. "He's like a bulldog, they say. Once he gets on your trail he never lets up."

Monk spat. "All we got to do is hold a pistol against this kid's head and Dillon will have to stop chasin' us."

"We've still got to keep ahead of him, hide the loot and get on into Pawnee. We can't risk splitting up now."

"You think we'll be safe in Pawnee?" asked the Kid.

"What the hell difference does that make?" asked Monk. "Dillon don't mean a goddamned thing in Pawnee. If he comes after us we can kill him and plead self-defense." He grinned. "Ain't nobody in Pawnee goin' to testify it was anything else."

"There's still the Law and Order group to consider," said Mark thoughtfully. "They just might stand up to Grant and make it stick. You've got to think of that, too."

"We can take care of them easy enough," boasted the Kid.

Manton shook his head. "Those days are about over in Pawnee," he said quickly. He looked back again. "Which means also that we've got to get rid of Dillon *before* he finds us in Pawnee."

"Maybe we could double back and head for Oklahoma, Texas and the Mexican border," said Monk brightly.

"No," said Mark. "By this time that telegraph line has been repaired and telegrams have been sent out in all directions. Dillon is too smart a lawman to overlook that. He's also too smart not to push on after us right now to keep us moving, wearing out our horses and not being able to get any rest. And, in a day or so, these prairies will be alive with posses."

"I don't think it looks so good," said Monk. Monk had always relied on his guns, knife, boots and fists to work his way through a troublesome life. Trying to outthink an enemy was completely out of his bracket.

"I'll get us out of this," said Manton, "but you've got to obey my orders to the letter. We're going to fight a rear-guard action in the little time we've got left before the law covers these prairies with a network we'd never break through and which even Ned Grant couldn't save us from."

"You do the talking, Mark," agreed the Kid.

"Yeah," said Monk.

"Just before the dawn the Kid will drop out at a good spot and get off the trail. If Dillon is still trailing us, it will be up to the Kid to kill their horses. Get off the trail about two hundred yards so that the sun is rising behind you, Kid. Get in your shots and then get to hell out of there. Don't wait around to see what a great marksman you've been! And, for Christ's sake, if you wound any of the men don't go in to finish them off. Remember that!"

It was just about dawn when Dillon and Newly, leading their spare horses, saw a thick bosque up ahead of them through which ran a shallow creek. Its course was plainly marked by a fringe of willows and cottonwoods.

"It's a natural for an ambush," said Matt. He uncased his fieldglasses to study the bosque.

The Laredo Kid lay at a right angle to the trail, about two hundred fifty yards to the east, well-sited behind a low roll of the ground fringed with tufts of buffalo grass. He wet a finger to find the direction of the faint dawn wind. He raised the buckhorn rear sight of his Winchester '73 and then cuddled his cheek against the stock, placing his finger against the trigger. He took up the trigger slack, sighted on one of the two led horses, took in a deep breath and then squeezed the trigger. The .44/40 slug hit the horse in the head and it dropped to the ground, dead.

The Kid quickly levered a fresh round into the chamber of the Winchester, took another sight at the second led horse and dropped it with a bullet through the right front leg, breaking it cleanly.

Newly dropped the lead rope of his spare horse and yanked his Winchester from the saddle bucket. He aimed at the gunsmoke drifting over a low roll in the ground perhaps 250 yards to the east and against the rising sun. He fired just as the Kid fired at Newly's own horse. The horse reared and the slug passed clean into Newly's right forearm, breaking the bones. Newly cursed as he dropped his rifle and swung down from the saddle, pain shooting through his body.

Matt Dillon jerked out his Winchester and fired as fast as he could at the drifting gunsmoke along the ground roll. The continuous echoes of gun reports chased each other along the prairie.

The Kid was gone. He had bellied back to an arroyo where he had ground-reined his buckskin. He led the buckskin, running lightly on foot out of sight of Dillon and his deputy until he was far out of range. Then he mounted, spurring off to join Mark and Monk, and the boy, who were miles ahead.

Matt Dillon quickly refilled his rifle magazine. "He's gone by now," he said over his shoulder. He walked to the softly cursing Newly and looked at the bleeding arm. He pressed on a lump under the skin and the flattened bullet dropped to the ground. "I'll have to set the bone," he said. "We'd better get under cover in the bosque. That dry-gulcher might still be around."

When the sun was fully up, Matt finished splinting the reset arm bones. He wiped the sweat from his brow and looked into Newly's pale face. He uncorked a flask and handed it to Newly. "This is on me," he said. He watched the deputy drink.

Newly lowered the flask, wiped his mouth on his left arm sleeve and looked back at the two dead horses. "Looks like we're finished," he said. "We're stopped cold."

Matt shook his head. "Not me," he said. "I'm going

on. You'll have to go back to Dodge and get Doc to take care of that arm."

"You're all alone now, Matt. Your horse is worn out. The led horses are dead."

Matt shrugged. "That's the way it goes sometimes," he said philosophically. "And stopping's just what they expect me to do."

Newly started back to the south while Matt watered his horse and made a quick pot of coffee. When he was ready he led the big gray on foot, while he studied the wet ground. Up until they had fired upon the led horses, Matt hadn't been too sure that he and Newly were on the right trail. He had been working purely on instinct. It was tough that the cost of making sure had cost him his deputy and the two led horses, but he knew that by the time Festus and the posse showed up, unless he stayed on the trail, it would be a cold trail indeed.

The morning wind brought the faint rataplan of distant rifle fire to Mark Manton and Monk Cole in a bosque where they had stopped to see the effect of the Kid's ambush.

"Matt Dillon will find you and arrest you," warned Billy Gaines.

Monk grinned. "You hear that rifle-fire, kid?" he asked. "That means your Matt Dillon has likely got a bullet in that thick head of his."

"No," said the boy. "I heard you men talking about killing only the led horses. You wouldn't dare shoot Matt. Kill a lawman and every other lawman in the territory would be after you."

Mark and Monk led the horses into a stream and began to lead them downstream.

"You ain't going to fool Matt Dillon by making these horses walk in the stream," jeered Billy.

"You got a big mouth, kid," warned Monk.

"He'll round up you crooks and hang you from a tele-graph pole," Billy warned.

"Listen to him," growled Monk.

Mark Manton climbed the bank and looked south. He could see the Kid riding across country, aiming to meet them at the rendezvous they had planned ahead. "It's the Kid," he said over his shoulder.

They met the Kid at a remote homesteader's place. A silent farmer took their tired horses and gave them fresh ones, as pre-arranged by Mark some weeks past. The Kid reported what had happened at his ambush.

"So now it's Dillon alone following us," mused Mark.

"We've thrown him off the trail," said Monk.

Mark shook his head. "No," he said quietly. "But I expected this." He looked at the farmer. "You keep those horses out of sight. If a lawman comes by here asking questions, you don't know anything. Understand? Tell him *nothing!* You understand that clearly?"

The man nodded. His worn face was enigmatic. He watched them as they rode east on the rutted road, leaving plenty of tracks in the fresh mud. He shifted the straw in his mouth from one side to the other. "East, hell," he said. He spat.

Five miles beyond the farm they led the horses across a rock outcropping and then into a shallow stream that trended north and east.

"Ain't we supposed to hide the loot somewhere around here?" asked Monk.

"Are you loco?" Mark said. "They can make that loudmouth Barney talk back there in Dodge." He shook his head. "Besides, that's where Ned Grant expects us to cache the loot."

"So?" asked Monk.

"Didn't it ever occur to you that if we ride into Paw-nee without the loot there isn't a single damned thing we could do about it if Ned decides he wants all the money for himself? We might not last five minutes if he thinks that way."

"I never thought of that," said Monk.

"*I* did," said Mark.

"Always one jump ahead, eh, Mark?" asked the Kid.

A faint light came into Monk's little eyes. "Yeah," he said slowly. "I get it now."

"You're getting smarter by the minute," said the Kid.

"I ain't stupid!" said Monk angrily.

"Not much, you ain't," said Billy.

Monk looked slowly at Billy. "Come to think of it," he said, "if we do hide the loot somewheres else other than where Ned figures we will, that kid there will be around to see where we do it."

"That's the money from my father's bank," said Billy. "It don't belong to him. It belongs to the people of Dodge. Some of them are poor people. It may be all they got saved up."

Monk shaped a cigarette. "Listen to him," he said drily.

The sun was fully up now, warming the great prairie. Mark Manton led the way north at top speed, urging on the fresh horses to put distance between themselves and Matt Dillon. In the early afternoon they reached a brook that meandered through a wood. The horses were tiring.

They led the horses into the shelter of the wood and Mark Manton took his fieldglasses and returned to the edge of the trees. He studied the sun-brightened terrain to the south. There was no one in sight. He handed the glasses to Monk. "Your turn to stay behind and make a welcome for Dillon—that is, if he gets this far." He grinned at the others.

"Ain't we going to hide the loot?" asked Monk.

The Kid was standing behind Monk looking at Mark. He winked.

"Not until you catch up with us," replied Mark.

"How do I know that?" demanded Monk.

The Kid walked up beside Monk and smiled his most engaging smile. "I'll see to it, Monk," he said pleasantly. "You trust us, don't you?"

"I ain't so sure," said Monk.

"Look," continued the Kid. "Sid is gone now, poor fella, and that stupid Barney is sitting in the cooler at Dodge. We don't have to share the loot with them now, do we? Maybe we won't even have to share the loot with Grant. You know how much money that ought'a be for each of us? Say, about $65,000! That's a helluva lot better than what Grant would have handed us after we took all the risks, eh?"

"I never thought of that," said Monk.

"But, if Dillon catches up with us, none of us will get a damned cent out of the deal. Nothing except a hemp necktie. Right?"

Monk nodded slowly.

"You're sure now you can take care of Dillon?" asked the Kid. He grinned. "He's some tough nut, Monk. Maybe tougher even than you."

"The hell he is! You want me to prove it?"

The Kid nodded. "You do that, Monk."

The Kid and Mark Manton led the horses from the woods. The Kid slanted his eyes toward Mark. Mark smiled back. Monk's stupidity was reliable. That's what they were counting on now.

Monk sat with his back against a tree in a place where the sun warmed him. Now and again he yawned. The sun was pleasant after the cold, rainy night through which he had passed. Once in a while he would raise the fieldglasses and look out over the pleasant, rolling terrain. There was a warm wind blowing, waving the buffalo grass so that it looked like the rippling waters of the sea. Birds twittered cheerily in the trees. Monk yawned.

Matt Dillon led his horse into the barnyard of the ramshackle homestead farm. A lean, saturnine man lounged out from behind the barn, saying nothing, chewing on a straw.

Matt showed his badge. "Dillon," he said. "United States Marshal. I'm looking for three men and a boy. The men are wanted for murder, kidnapping and bank robbery."

The man shrugged. "I don't know nothing."

A slatternly woman came out of the kitchen doorway of the house. A small, runny-nosed child clung to her skirts.

"Tall dark man," added Dillon. "Thick-bodied man. Younger man, always smiling, light hair, blue eyes. Boy about ten years old. Freckled face. Reddish hair. Big for his age."

"Ain't seen them," said the farmer.

"There are a lot of hoof and boot marks here in the mud," said Matt.

"There usually are."

"Hired help?" asked Matt. He looked at the barn. "Mind if I look in there?"

"Sure do, marshal! You got no business in my place."

"Aaron!" called out the woman. "You let that man go in there if he wants and you tell him the truth!"

Matt looked at Aaron. "If I go in that barn and find their horses which you may have exchanged for fresh ones, I can hold you for aiding and abetting, and as accessory after the fact."

"What the hell does that mean?"

"It means you'll go to jail and stand trial along with them if they're caught!" shrilled the woman.

"She's right," said Matt. "Now, if you'll admit you helped those men and held horses for them here, and you tell me which way they went, I'll forget you were involved."

Aaron silently opened the barn door. Matt saw the mud-plastered, exhausted horses. They were the same horses he had stampeded earlier that morning in the alleyway behind the Dodge City Bank, and which later the outlaws had ridden from the town. There was another horse in the barn, a scrubby-looking, ungroomed roan. Matt pointed at it. "You'll take that gray of mine in exchange for the roan?"

"I ain't got much choice."

"You're getting the best of the deal," said Matt. He shifted his saddle and led the roan out.

The woman held out a cup of coffee and a thick sandwich to Matt. "They went east," she said. "Said they was goin' 'o Larned, but I didn't believe them."

"Hell," said the farmer.

Matt looked at him. "Where would you go around here if you were on the run?"

"Five miles east on the road. Rock outcropping to the left. Lead my horse over that. Stream on the north side of it. Lead the horse up or down the stream a mile or so, then get out."

Matt nodded. "Thanks," he said.

Matt later led his roan over the rock outcropping to the stream. He followed the stream until he found the tracks on the northern bank and he followed them across the prairie.

In the late afternoon Matt scouted a thick woods ahead of him with his fieldglasses. The bright sun reflected off something in the dark woods. Matt led his roan out of sight into the woods and tethered it. He faded into a gully and worked his way around behind the trees.

Monk was sleeping peacefully. He slowly opened his eyes. Something was wrong. The birds had stopped twittering in the trees. He carefully placed his hand on his Winchester.

"Keep your hands away from that rifle," warned Dillon

from fifty feet behind Monk. "Stand up. Grab your ears! *Pronto!*"

Monk made his play, surprisingly fast for a man of his bulk. He threw himself sideways, drawing out his six-shooter, rolling over and over and firing each time he came upright.

Matt fanned off three slugs. The .44/40's hit the man in the head and he rolled over for the last time and lay still.

The firing echoes drifted off into the silence of the sunny prairies. The wind rustled the grass. It was suddenly very, very quiet.

Matt looked through Monk's pockets. There was no money in them except for a few coins and a five dollar bill. He led Monk's horse to the roan and then checked the saddlebags. None of the bank loot was in them. He mounted the roan and led Monk's horse north.

The wind had carried the sound of rifle-firing to Mark Manton and the Kid as they rested in a bosque.

The Kid grinned. "Well, likely old Monk got Dillon's horse."

Mark wasn't sure. "A lot of firing to kill one horse," he said quietly.

"Maybe Monk killed Dillon?"

"Maybe it's the other way around."

"Ain't nobody can kill Matt Dillon!" cried Billy.

"I'd like to try," said the Kid. "Maybe I'd better wait here and see."

Mark shrugged. "Suits me," he said.

The Kid rested his hand on his Colt. "Split the loot," he said quietly. "I want my share now."

"That's loco!" said Mark. "We've got to stick together on this thing!"

The Kid shook his head. "I'm not going back to Pawnee and if you had any sense at all neither would you."

"By tomorrow every lawman in the state will know bout us!"

"I'll take that risk," said the Kid.

Mark jerked open the saddlebag closest to him. He brought out the bank money in taped blocks. He swiftly began to separate it into two piles.

"That's fifty-fifty, ain't it?" asked the Kid.

Mark nodded as he counted.

"No go," said the Kid.

Mark slowly turned. He'd never be able to beat the Kid at a fast draw. "What the hell are you talking about?" he demanded. "It's equal shares, isn't it?"

The Kid grinned. "You forgot about poor ol' Monk," he said. "I got to look out for his interest, don't I?"

"If that gunfire was Dillon killing Monk," said Mark. "We're damned fools standing around here arguing about shares."

The Kid swiftly drew his Colt and cocked it. "Two-thirds goes my way. Count it out!"

Mark counted it out. He dumped the Kid's and Monk's share at the Kid's feet. "You want to itemize it?" he sneered.

The Kid smiled. "I trust you, *amigo*."

"It's for you and Monk, you know."

"Sure. Sure. Good ol' Monk."

Mark mounted his horse and picked up the lead rope of Billy's horse. "See you in hell!" he snarled. He spurred the horse.

The Laredo Kid teetered back and forth on his boot-heels as he squatted in the bright sunshine, completely absorbed in counting out the money. "Jesus, oh, sweet Jesus," he muttered. He never heard Mark Manton as he catfooted up behind him with a pair of empty saddlebags hung over his left forearm and with a cocked Colt in his

right hand. There was one crisp, sharp pistol report. Mart
Manton stepped over the dead body, gathered up the
money and stuffed it into the saddlebags and then ran
swiftly off into the shadows of the woods.

Matt Dillon had lost the trail. He quartered back and
forth, leaning from the saddle to look for tracks. He heard
a faint and distant gun report. He worked his way slowly
and carefully toward the sound of the shot.

The Laredo Kid lay face downward on the ground with
a bullet hole behind his right ear. Matt Dillon rolled him
over by thrusting a big boot toe under the body. A single
dollar bill was clutched in the Kid's stiffening right hand.

Chapter 13

It was late evening in Pawnee. The street lamps sputtered fitfully in the cold wind that swept in from the prairies. Ned Grant paced back and forth in his suite in the Grant Hotel, with an unlighted Grant Stogie in his mouth. Sheriff Lem Martin stood at the corner window in the suite looking down lamplighted Grant Street toward the Pawnee River bridge. The telegram from Festus lay on the marble-topped table, recently brought to Ned Grant by the sheriff.

"Where the hell are they?" demanded Grant. "What happened to Barney? There was no mention of him in the telegram. Where the hell is all that money?"

Lem looked back at him, wondering which was more important to Ned—the money looted from the Dodge City Bank or Barney. It was an interesting thought. Until Lem had brought the telegram to Ned Grant, he had had no knowledge of the bank job. Lem had a sneaking suspicion that somehow Barney must have fouled up the raid. It wasn't like Mark Manton and the others to do so.

Ned paced back and forth. "They got away with the money—at least three of them did, according to the telegram, but there is no mention of Barney. What the hell could have happened?"

"And the kid they took," added Lem. "Billy Gaines. You don't suppose they'd be stupid enough to get rid of the kid?"

Ned stopped pacing. "You mean *kill* him?"

Lem shrugged. "They're a desperate bunch now, Ned
Running like hell with all that money and with ever
lawman in Kansas warned about them. According to th
telegram, Matt Dillon and a deputy are close behind them
You know Dillon. He'll never give up once he gets on th
trail. My guess is that he'll keep on their tails, keepin
them moving all the time and not giving them a chanc
to stop and think."

"My God," said Ned. "I never thought of them killin
that kid."

Lem looked quickly at him. It wasn't like Ned Gran
to worry himself about any kid but his own.

"They'd put all our necks into a noose."

Lem nodded. It was the old Ned speaking now, con
cerned only about himself. "Not *mine,*" he said quietly
"But yours . . . If your boys squeal, Ned, they'll tal
plenty about you planning this thing."

Ned relighted his cigar. "It was such a sure thing," h
muttered around the cigar. "What could have gon
wrong?"

Someone tapped on the door. The handle turned an
Mark Manton came into the room. He locked the doo
behind himself.

Ned Grant paled. "What the hell are you doing here?"
he demanded. "Do you know what you've done? You'r
leading every lawman in Kansas straight to Pawnee an
me."

Mark walked to the side table and poured a doubl
slug of Grant's Special Blend. He gulped it down and
then turned. *"You?"* he asked. "Where the hell else coul
I have gone? Dillon would have cut us off to the south
east and west. We would have been rounded up within
twenty-four hours and maybe strung up to boot fo
what happened back in Dodge."

"Where's the money? Where's Barney?" demanded Ned

"You should ask him where Dillon is," said Lem drily.

"What about your men?" snarled Mark. "Don't you give a damn about *them,* Grant? Sid Kellar, Monk Cole and the Kid?"

"Well, what about them?" asked Grant.

Manton refilled his glass and downed it. He wiped his mouth with the back of a shaking hand. "They're dead," he said huskily. "Barney was captured in Dodge. Sid shot to pieces leaving the bank. Monk and the Kid killed by Dillon when he was trailing us north."

"Dillon?" snapped Grant. "Where is he?"

"You're likely to see him riding right up Grant Street any minute," replied Mark.

"He was *that* close behind you?"

Mark nodded. He felt for his tobacco and papers and shaped a cigarette with shaking hands.

"The kid, Mark?" asked Lem.

Mark waved a hand. "I let him go early this afternoon. I didn't want to bring him here. He had served his purpose. Dillon will likely pick him up."

"The money?" asked Grant.

"Hidden in the cache," lied Mark.

"Who else knows about it?"

"Just me," Mark ran his tongue along the edge of the cigarette paper but kept his dark eyes on Grant. "I blindfolded and tied up the kid before I stashed the loot."

"Then you're the only one, besides me, who knows where it is?" asked Grant.

Mark lighted his cigarette, watching Ned over the flare of the match. He fanned out the match. "And Barney," he added. He studied Ned.

"In jail in Dodge," said Ned quietly. He wiped his sweating face. "Supposing he talks?" asked Ned tensely. It was almost as though he was talking to himself.

There were no answers from the others.

"It was Barney who messed things up," said Mark

relentlessly. "I never wanted to take him along. He's useless, drunken fool, Ned. If it hadn't been for *him* w would have made the hit and gotten away scot free."

"Shut up!" snapped Ned. "I don't want to hear it!"

"You *will,*" persisted Mark. "That damned kid move away from his assigned post and allowed Dillon t stampede our horses and then kill Sid as he was leavin the rear door of the bank. It was Dillon who got you precious Barney. The only way we salvaged the raid wa to take the boy as hostage. Another thing: it was you wh assured me that Dillon would be out of town. Even wit Barney messing things up we might have gotten awa with it if Dillon hadn't shown up."

"How the hell would I know that?" demanded Ned He turned and looked at Lem Martin. "You'd better ar range for a reception for Dillon," he added.

"Like what?" asked the sheriff. "You don't suppose I' be stupid enough to try to kill him here in Pawnee, d you?"

"Think of something! I didn't give you that job fo nothing!"

"I've been wondering just what kind of job you hav given me. You didn't let me in on this Dodge City raid not that it matters to me now. I wouldn't want any par of it."

"You know who you're talking to?" demanded Grant

Lem nodded. "A man who is a has-been. You're jus about through here in Pawnee, Ned. Dillon will tie yo in with the Dodge City deal as sure as you're standin there. Barney is likely to talk to save his own butt. I can' say that I'd blame him."

Ned paled. "What do you think I should do?"

Lem shrugged. "I'd get out of Pawnee as fast as could and I'd keep on going, say to Mexico."

Mark Manton glanced quickly sideways at Ned.

"Go on," said Ned.

"I'd get down to Dodge while Dillon is up this way and most of the lawmen of Kansas were looking around this way. I'd spring Barney out of jail while I had the chance. I'll hold Dillon here to give you a chance."

"That's real fine of you, Lem!" said Ned.

Lem smiled. "At a price," he quietly added.

"Such as?"

Lem looked out of the window. "General power of attorney over any *legal* properties you have here in Pawnee."

"You know how much that could be?"

Lem slowly nodded. "I have a good idea. I know I'll never get away with *all* of it, because the state will have the courts impound it once they know where you are and what you've done. But, I'll have time enough to get *something* out of it."

"A helluva lot!" snapped Ned.

"Maybe." Lem walked to the door. He turned. "Do I get it?" he asked.

"And if you don't?"

"Then I tell Dillon where you are and that you know where the bank money is hidden, and that you aim to spring Barney from the Dodge City jail. Then Dillon will send a telegram down there warning them about what you plan to do. You'll never free Barney and you'll either end up dead, or in the jail with him. You have no choice, Ned."

"You scheming sonofabitch!" cried Ned.

"You'd have done the same thing to me," said Lem, "and you've operated that way around here for the past ten years or so."

"You'll hold Dillon then?"

"As long as I can, perhaps twenty-four hours. *Incommunicado.*"

"You'll have to do it, Ned," said Mark. "You were planning to leave Pawnee anyway."

Ned nodded. "Go downstairs and round up abou
five of the *corrida*. Pick the best of them. I'll offer them
a thousand dollars apiece to help me spring Barney. Ge
a pair of horses for me and a pair for you. Each man i
to have two mounts. It will be a straight ride through't
Dodge City."

Mark started for the door.

"Mark," said Ned.

Mark turned.

"You take off now, by yourself, and I'll have those
same five men hunt you down, or I'll have Lem Martin
here arrest you, and you'll never leave his jail alive. You
understand?"

Mark nodded. He closed the door behind himself. Ned
Grant had read his mind.

Ned sat down and took a legal form from his desk. He
looked at Lem Martin. "Go get Anson Crowder," he
said. "He'll have to notarize this."

When Lem left to get the justice of the peace, Ned
Grant slid aside a wall picture and quickly opened a wall
safe. He removed some bundles of cash, always held in
reserve for such an anticipated emergency and placed the
money in a small handbag. He swiftly changed into trail
clothing and swung a gunbelt about his waist. He holstered
a Colt and slid a double-barreled Derringer into his coat
pocket. By the time Lem Martin returned with Anson
Crowder, Ned had already filled out the general power of
attorney. He managed to keep a straight face all the time
the deal was going on, as Lem Martin certainly could not
know that *all* of the properties which Ned was virtually
signing over to him were soon to be investigated by the
state authorities. Ned Grant would be well out of it by
then.

Lem Martin looked out of the corner window when the
deal was completed. "Just in time, Ned," he said over hi

shoulder. "Matt Dillon is riding this way with a kid behind him."

Ned put on his hat. He ran to the door, then turned. "You'll keep your part of the deal?" he asked.

Lem waved the power of attorney. "Of course."

Ned closed the door.

They heard the rapid tattoo of his booted feet on the carpeted hallway.

"There goes a legend," said Anson Crowder thoughtfully.

"Good riddance," said Lem. He grinned. "Between the two of us, Anson, we can get some of the golden eggs the goose has been laying around here for Ned Grant these past ten years."

Matt Dillon dismounted in front of the sheriff's office. He lifted Billy Gaines from the saddle of the led horse. "You all right, Billy?" he asked.

"Sure," said Billy with a grin. "Are we going to run down Mark Manton now, Marshal Dillon?"

"I have my hopes," replied Matt. "But this is Pawnee, son, and it's home ground for men such as Mark Manton." Matt looked across the street. Two men were leaning against a lamp post watching him and Billy. He looked along the street on his side. To one side were three men standing on a street corner looking directly at him. To the other side two men stood in a doorway and they too were watching him. He looked across the street toward the Grant Hotel. A man stood behind a ground-floor window watching him and up on the second floor, in two different windows, were other men watching him. Dillon instinctively knew who they were—hardfaced men of the notorious Grant *corrida,* hired guns and deadly to any of Ned Grant's enemies.

"You're Matt Dillon, aren't you?" a man asked Matt. "I am."

"You've got your nerve coming into Pawnee, Marshal Dillon."

Matt shrugged. "It's my business," he said.

"If you need any help, the Law and Order men will back your play."

Matt shook his head. "No need yet, mister. I don't want to get any of you involved unless it's absolutely necessary. Thanks anyway."

Matt and Billy walked into the sheriff's office. A deputy sat behind the desk. "I'm Matt Dillon," said Matt. "United States Marshal from the Dodge City area."

"Is that so?" asked the deputy.

"Is the sheriff here?" asked Matt.

"That's him coming through the doorway right behind you."

Matt turned to look into the smooth shaven, foxy-looking face of Lem Martin, a truly typical "political" law officer. "Did you receive a telegram from one of my deputies in reference to the bank robbery and the killings in Dodge City, and the fact that three men were wanted for those crimes?" asked Matt.

"I received a telegram," admitted Martin.

"Three of those men headed north this way. Two are now dead. The third man held this boy as hostage until earlier today, then left him and came here."

"So?" asked Martin.

"Have you seen him?"

Martin shook his head.

"The man is Mark Manton," said Matt.

"You're sure of that?"

"The boy knows who he is."

Martin walked around his desk and sat down in the chair vacated by his deputy. He looked at the boy. "You're sure he was Mark Manton, sonny?" he asked.

"Yes," replied Billy.

"How do you know he was?" continued Martin.

"I heard the others call him Mark," said Billy.

"Mark? Or Mark *Manton*?"

Billy looked up at Matt.

Matt leaned forward. "All this time we're wasting here may be allowing Manton to be putting miles between us and himself. Isn't it about time we did something about it?" he demanded.

Two men came into the office and leaned against the wall behind Matt.

The rear door of the office was opened and two more men came inside and past the cell block to stand behind Matt and Billy.

"You say you're Matt Dillon," said Lem Martin slowly.

Matt showed his badge. "I am," he said.

"Anyone can wear a badge and say he's a marshal." Lem reached into a pocket and took out the telegram he had received from Dodge City. "Now this here piece of paper is signed by somebody calling himself Matt Dillon."

"That telegram was sent by my orders from Festus, one of my deputies. I was on the trail of the bank robbers when it was sent."

Lem looked around at his hard faced men. "Well, that's something else, isn't it! Only we have no proof of that."

"Listen, sheriff," said Matt. "I don't know what your little game is . . ."

"Just explain to me how you managed to send a telegram from Dodge City early one morning and still be hot on the trail of these bank robbers? Pretty good trick, Dillon." Lem Martin laughed. His men laughed with him. Then Martin leaned forward. "Now, Mister Dillon, or whoever you are, I'm going to have to hold you here on possible charges of impersonating an officer of the law."

"That's ridiculous! There are people here who know me. Send a telegram to Dodge for verification of my presence here . . ." Matt's voice died away as he saw the look on Martin's smooth face.

"The boy will be taken care of," said Lem Martin. "I'll have your pistol now. Careful! I wouldn't want my men to get the idea you're drawing on me!"

Matt slowly drew his Colt from its holster and placed it on Martin's desk. "Look, Martin," he said quietly. "You're either making a big mistake or else you're getting paid to hold me here for some reason or another. Either way, you're obstructing justice and an officer in the performance of his duty."

Martin smiled smoothly. "Well, I hope you'll have witnesses at the time of the complaint, eh, men?"

"You're playing a dangerous game," warned Matt.

"I've played dangerous games all my life," countered Martin.

The cell door was closed and locked behind Matt.

Lem Martin took Billy by the arm. "Come with me, sonny," he said. "I'll see that you get a good dinner and a place to sleep for tonight. Your dad was here, but he left when he heard of the robbery. Tomorrow I'll notify the Dodge City authorities that you're here."

"Why not tonight?" called Matt from his cell.

"The telegraph office doesn't open until eight in the morning," lied Martin.

"You can have it opened for official business," said Matt.

But the door had closed behind Lem Martin and little Billy.

It wasn't until half-past ten o'clock the next morning that the Dodge City posse, nine men led by Festus, was riding toward Pawnee when two horsemen came riding up at fulll gallop, dust whirling in their wake, about two miles out of town. Festus held up his hand and the posse came to a halt.

"I'm Kelly Byrnes," said a rider, "and this is Forbes

Caskill. We're both local men. Are you the Dodge City posse?"

"We are," said Festus.

"One of the men you were following reached here yesterday evening, name of Mark Manton. Marshal Matt Dillon arrived after he did and was arrested on false charges and thrown into the jail by Sheriff Lem Martin."

"You don't say!" cried Festus. "That must be some sheriff yuh have."

"You don't have to remind us," said Caskill grimly. "Dillon had a little boy with him, name of Billy Gaines."

Festus nodded. "Banker Gaines' son. He was taken as hostage by the bank robbers. Poor little fella! Is he all right?"

"Yes, he's fine. They wouldn't dare do a thing to him."

"What's the purpose of the false arrest?" asked Festus.

"We believe Ned Grant, Mark Manton and four or five of Grant's other hired guns rode south last night, and that Martin arrested Dillon to keep him from getting on their trail."

Festus touched his horse with his spurs. "Well," he said. "Let's get on into Pawnee and get Matthew out of the cooler so's he can get a telegram off about Grant and Manton."

"Wait," said Kelly Byrnes. "Lem Martin is a Grant man. There are still plenty of Grant's *corrida* in and around Pawnee to make it damned hot for anyone coming into town."

"That don't bother us," said Festus.

"We want no gunplay in Pawnee," said Byrnes. "We're representing the Law and Order people of Pawnee. Without us to help you, you'd be outnumbered. Without you, we won't have the strength to take over the town. Together, we can get done what both of us must do—you to get Dillon, and us to get control of Pawnee."

"Sounds fair enough," said Festus. "Let's go!"

Forbes Caskill went ahead to alert the Law and Order men. Festus and Byrnes gave him half an hour to do so.

Slowly, almost imperceptibly, the Law and Order men filtered into the streets from their places of business—stores, shops, offices and mills. None of them outwardly carried weapons, as opposed to the swaggering men of the *corrida,* none of whom knew that Ned Grant had left Pawnee forever.

It was after eleven o'clock that the alert passed from one *corrida* man to another and then to Lem Martin that the Dodge City posse was clattering over the plank bridge that crossed the Pawnee River. The *corrida* men fanned out to their positions at strategic points along Grant Street. None of them noticed that for every *corrida* man there was a Law and Order man within a short distance, but not too observable. In any case, the *corrida* men were not looking out for the Law and Order men, most of whom they despised as weak "townies." They kept their hard eyes on the Dodge City men who rode into Grant Street loose and easy in the saddle, despite the fact that they had ridden many hard miles to reach Pawnee.

Festus drew rein outside of the sheriff's office. He pretended not to notice that the men of the *corrida* had closed in behind the posse, who had dismounted. Lem Martin came out of the office into the bright sunlight.

Festus nodded politely. "The name is Festus," he said. "Deputy marshal from Dodge. I was told to report to Marshal Matt Dillon here in Pawnee."

"Marshal Dillon is being held here, if he *is* Marshal Dillon," replied Martin. *"Incommunicado,"* he added.

Festus nodded. "So I've heard. Well, now, I can identify him, Sheriff. Just show this man to me."

Martin smiled smoothly. He looked beyond Festus and the lounging posse to see his own men surrounding the Dodge group. "And who can identify *you?*" he asked Festus pleasantly.

Festus opened his coat and showed the badge pinned to his vest.

Martin slowly shook his head. "I can buy a badge like that in any hock shop in Kansas City," he said.

Festus pursed his lips. He looked around slowly. Stern-faced townsmen were closing in behind the men of the *corrida*. Kelly Byrnes was with them and Forbes Caskill stood in the door of his gunshop with his hands behind his back. "So, you won't let me see the marshal?" asked Festus.

"No," said Martin.

Festus waved a hand to Kelly Byrnes. Each of the Law and Order men drew his pistol. Forbes Caskill walked out into the sunlit street with a double-barreled shotgun held in his hands.

"Look behind you!" warned Martin.

The *corrida* men whirled, dropping their hands to their gun belts.

"All right, boys," said Festus.

The lounging posse straightened up and jerked Winchesters from their saddle scabbards, levering rounds of .44/40 cartridges into the rifle chambers. The *corrida* men whirled as they heard the lever actions being worked and looked across the rifle barrels into the hard faces of the Dodge City posse.

Festus smiled pleasantly at Martin. "I'll see Matt Dillon now," he said.

Martin released Matt and handed him his Colt. "It was all a mistake, Dillon," he said.

"It sure was, Martin," drawled Festus. "Yours . . ."

Matt Dillon wasted no time. "We'll need fresh horses, two to a man," he said. "Manton and Grant have a fifteen hour start on us. Send your men separately throughout the town, Festus, to see if they can find out which way Manton and Grant went. Get over to the telegraph office and get warning messages out. Send one man to get food for the posse. As soon as we can get an idea of which way they went we'll leave Pawnee. I don't have much faith in the fact that we might catch up with them, but there's nothing else we can do. My bet is that they've gone south and might want to pick up Barney on the way."

"Yuh mean bust him out'a the jail?" asked Festus. He shook his head.

"You've forgotten that the only man at the jail now is Newly, with a broken arm to boot. Every other deputy is here with us. Make sure the first message out is for Dodge City."

Kelly Byrnes shook his head. "There's no direct line to Dodge," he said. "The message will have to be sent east to Salina and then relayed to Wichita, and then to Dodge. It will likely take hours."

"It's the best we can do," said Matt. "Let's hope it gets to Dodge City before Grant and Manton do."

It was half-past twelve when one of the possemen brought the news that Ned Grant, Mark Manton and five other men had been seen riding south on the road to High Springs late the night before. By one o'clock Matt Dillon was leading the Dodge City posse south on the High Springs Road.

Chapter 14

A full harvest moon hung over the valley of the Arkansas River as Ned Grant, Mark Manton and the five *corrida* men drew rein in a woods that stood to the north of Dodge City and through which passed the main north-south road. They dismounted and watered their horses from a small stream that meandered through the woods on its way to the Arkansas.

"When do we go in?" asked Cal Barnett, one of the *corrida* men.

Ned Grant lighted a cigar. "As soon as possible," he replied.

"With that moon?" asked Ken Dart. He jerked a thumb toward the great bright orb that flooded the countryside with pale silvery light.

Grant took out his pocket watch and pressed the button. The fine watch struck twelve. "We can't just sit around here waiting for darkness to come," said Ned. "Maybe Lem Martin wasn't able to hold Dillon back. Dillon might be right on our trail now. He might catch up with us at any time."

"One man," sneered Jim Downer. He laughed. "You act like Dillon was God Almighty himself."

Ned looked casually at the *corrida* man. "Did it ever occur to you that Dillon's posse might have caught up with him at Pawnee? That he could have already sent out telegrams alerting the people in Dodge? That he might have left Pawnee not long after us?"

Cal Betz looked toward the north along the moon-lit road. "Ned's got a point there," he said. "Let's get this over with."

"I'm with Cal," put in Jack Harding. "Let's make the hit, get Barney, get the hell out of Dodge and scatter before Dillon shows up. It's a cinch I ain't goin' back to Pawnee now."

"Mark?" asked Ned. He studied Manton, who had been very quiet during the long, hard ride south.

Mark nodded. "Let's get it over with," he said.

"Tell them what to do," Ned ordered.

Mark took out the same map that had been made for the bank raid. He spread it out on a stump. The moon-light was bright enough so that it could be plainly seen. "Here's the marshal's office," he explained. He placed a finger on it. "There will probably be only one man there at this time of the night. The front door opens on the main street. The rear door opens on an alleyway and across the alleyway is a row of sheds, stables and so forth. Along the main street on either side of the office and across the street from it, for some blocks are nothing but business establishments, so there likely won't be anyone in any of them."

"What about the saloons?" asked Ken Dart.

"It's a week-night," said Mark. "Most of them close up if there isn't enough business to warrant keeping them open. Even so, we won't have to worry about a bunch of drunks and some stupid bartenders giving us any trou-ble. If we can keep quiet going into the town and cover the approaches to the jail, we'll be able to make our get-away without any problems. We'll get into the office by a ruse, take care of whoever is in charge there, spring Barney and get out of town before anyone is alerted. We know that Dillon's two deputies can't give us much trouble; Festus is likely in Pawnee right now leading the Dodge City posse. Newly got wounded by the Laredo Kid when he was following our trail from Dodge and Dillon must have sent him back, because he was alone when he got to Pawnee.

"Now, we station a man here, at the junction of the rear alleyway behind the marshal's office and the next street, to cover anyone coming that way. At the other end of the alleyway we station one man who will hold the horses ready for us and keep an eye out for anyone coming from that direction. At the main intersection of the town, a short distance from the front of the marshal's office, we station another man to watch both ways for anyone approaching. Down the street, where the alleyway behind the marshal's office opens onto the main north-south street, another man is posted.

"One man goes to the office door and asks whoever is in charge there for help. Once he gets into the office and distracts the attention of the deputy, another man comes in behind him and silences him. They open the rear door of the office and let Ned in. Barney is freed. The front door of the office is locked. The escape is made through the rear door and down the alleyway to the horses. Then we break out of Dodge and out of Kansas. For God's sake, don't anyone try for the bridge if there is pursuit because it hasn't been repaired."

The *corrida* men nodded. Ned Grant studied the map and then nodded too. "Should work," he said. He looked at Mark. "Show these men their posts."

Mark looked around. "All right?" They nodded. "I'll stay with the horses," added Mark. "I had enough shooting when we hit the bank here. I think I'm entitled to the post."

"Then it's settled," said Ned. "Each of you take a close look at the chart. You've all been in Dodge at one time or another so you're familiar with the layout of the town.

Each of you pick out the way you'll go when you leave. Once the raid is over we split and we'll probably never see each other again."

Grant walked to one of his two horses and took a roll of bills from a saddlebag. He paid each of the *corrida* members and added an extra five hundred dollars as a bonus. "One thing," he said. "Shoot to kill if there's any interference. None of us wants to be recognized. They'll know who made the raid all right, but if anything happens in the future about this thing, they won't have any witnesses. If any of you are hit and can't escape, that's your problem. Once the jail break is made each man is on his own."

Mark Manton walked to his two horses. He tightened the straps on the full cantle roll he had. He withdrew his Winchester from its saddle scabbard and checked it for a full load. He replaced it in the scabbard and then opened the loading gate of his Colt. He twirled the cylinder, checking the six chambers to see if they were loaded.

"You'll ride with me and Barney when we leave Dodge," said Ned Grant.

Mark made no indication of his surprise as he turned. "Sure," he said.

"We won't head for the loot right away," added Ned. "That would be too obvious. We'll head for Mexico and lay low for about a year, then come north and get it."

"Good thought," said Mark. He shaped a cigarette and placed it in his mouth. Ned Grant was quick to light a lucifer and hold it to the tip of Mark's cigarette. His hard eyes held the other man's. "So don't get any ideas of taking off on your own," he said.

Mark shook his head. "I know better than to try that, Ned. I'd have everything to lose and nothing to gain. Besides, now that the other Four Horsemen are gone, that gives us a bigger share."

Ned nodded. "Three ways," he said. "Not equal, of course."

"You mean Barney?"

"I mean you."

Mark slowly took the cigarette from his mouth. "But why?" he asked.

"I made the set-up in Coahuila. I did all the arranging for the bank robbery in Dodge. And, Manton, I'm still the boss. Just remember that." He turned on his heel and walked back to his other men.

Mark watched Grant. He leaned back against his saddled horse and rested an arm atop the full saddle roll where his blanket and slicker were neatly wrapped around two hundred thousand or more dollars. He smiled faintly. "Further, Manton, I'm still the boss," he mimicked. He laughed softly to himself.

The horses were watered and the saddles shifted from the tired animals to the fresher ones. No one spoke. Last cigarettes were shaped and smoked. Winchesters and Colts were checked again. Bandannas were turned around so that they could be drawn up to cover noses.

The moon was slanting down to the west. There would be some shadows now in the streets of Dodge City.

"We'll go in one at a time and take our positions," instructed Ned Grant.

One by one at five minute intervals each man rode toward Dodge City, dreaming in the dying moonlight.

Chapter 15

The Long Branch emptied out earlier than usual that moonlit night. Hank Johnson passed among the empty tables and gathered the glasses. He watched Bert Quinn washing down the bar. Miss Kitty, pleading a headache, had gone upstairs to her rooms. The time had come, thought Hank, to finally deal with Quinn. Matt Dillon and Festus were out of town, hot on the trail of the bank robbers. Newly had returned to Dodge with his right arm in splints and a sling and had practically confined himself to the marshal's office, doing routine work and keeping an eye on Barney Grant.

Bert Quinn finished cleaning the bar. He took off his apron and walked into the storeroom. He had taken to carrying a short-barreled Colt in a half-breed holster under his left armpit ever since the appearance of the Four Horsemen and Barney Grant in Dodge. They were gone now, and Barney was in the cooler, but Ned Grant still had a long memory and a long arm and plenty of other hardcases in his *corrida*. Now that Dillon was out of town, there was no telling what Grant might do. Bert Quinn strapped on the holster and slid the Colt into it. It was made with the inner side open, but held shut by spring steel wire clips that held the pistol within the holster. But when the pistol was dragged sideways and down for a quick draw it passed easily through the open side of the holster. He put on his coat and hat and took the double-barreled Remington Derringer from his trousers pocket and put it into the left-hand pocket of his coat. He put on his hat and slanted it down over his spectacles. He looked at himself in the mirror over the washstand. A man can change inside, he thought, but he cannot greatly change his appearance. His expression can be changed, yes, but not his basic appearance.

"Ready to go?" asked Hank from the doorway.

Bert nodded. "It's a nice night for a walk," he said. "It's the only thing I don't like about this job, Hank. Being inside all the time."

"It does wear on a man," agreed Hank.

Bert looked at him. "You plan to stay on here, Hank?" he asked.

Hank shrugged. "I don't know," he said.

"You're well-liked here in the Long Branch and in Dodge City."

Hank walked into the storeroom and took off his apron. He took his gunbelt and holstered Colt from a hook and swung it about his lean waist with practiced ease. He buckled it and settled it about his hips.

"You're carrying a gun again, I see," observed Bert.

"I haven't forgotten what happened the night Barney Grant was in here. Besides, not carrying a gun in Dodge, a man feels half-naked."

Bert nodded. "You're right," he agreed. "I wish it was otherwise, and some day before too long it will be, but right now it's a simple form of life insurance."

They walked together to the front door. Bert closed it and locked it. He put the key into his pocket. "Wait," he said. He handed the key to Hank. "You're opening up in the morning."

Hank took the key. "That's right."

"You had forgotten?" asked Bert.

Hank looked sideways at Bert. Hank had not forgotten. He had not planned to be in Dodge at all the next day.

By the time the Long Branch should be opened Hank hoped to be miles away, headed west toward the Cimarron Country leaving Bert Quinn lying dead on the street somewhere in Dodge.

They crossed the main intersection of Dodge and paused on the street corner for a moment while Hank looked back along the street. For a fleeting moment he had thought he had seen a furtive movement out of the corner of his eye.

"What's the trouble?" asked Bert.

"Nothing," said Hank. I must be seeing things, he thought. What the hell is the matter with me, anyway? This should be easy. I owe this man nothing but a split skull and ten years of my life rotting in prison. I am his judge, jury, and will be finally his executioner. It is not only for myself I am going to do this, thought Hank, but also for the others who have suffered at the hands of this hard man. Oh, he had changed. There was no question about that, and he had truly saved Hank's life that night in the Long Branch when drunken Barney Grant had drawn on him. How much does one man really owe another for saving his life? Was ten years in prison and a ruined life a counterbalance for what Bert had done in the Long Branch?

"Hank?" asked Bert.

Hank turned, almost with a start.

Bert narrowed his eyes. There were times when he was almost sure that he had known this quiet, hardworking man somewhere back in the past of his checkered history. Had it been Pawnee? Bert had worked in and around Pawnee for well over ten years and Hank was really younger than he looked. Somewhere in his sad past the man had suffered and aged beyond his years. Yet Bert could not put a finger on the mental file of this man who called himself Hank Carson.

They walked together on the moonlit side of the

street. A lone horseman was down the street. He suddenly dismounted and hastily led his horse out of sight down an alleyway.

"Where do you suppose he's going?" asked Bert Quinn.

"Who knows?" said Hank.

A horse whinnied down the side alleyway to the right, beyond the marshal's office. The sound was faint, but they could hear it. Hank stopped and turned. There were too many people abroad on the streets of Dodge City for that time of the night, or maybe it was just his imagination, his tension at the thought of finally killing Bert Quinn.

A man coughed across the street, on the shadowed side.

Both Hank and Bert stopped and looked across the street. They could see a dark form in a shadowed doorway as though a man was standing motionless there.

"Look," said Bert softly.

Down the street a man walked quickly through a patch of the dying moonlight. The barrel of his rifle reflected in the pale glow.

"What the hell is going on?" muttered Bert.

"You're just nervous," said Hank. Then he smiled. "Can't say that I blame you. If I thought I knew Ned Grant's *corrida* men were looking for me, I suppose I'd be nervous, too."

Bert stopped walking and looked quickly sideways at Hank. "How did you know that?"

Hank smiled again. "Well, Barney Grant is Ned Grant's son, isn't he? He wouldn't be quick to forget about what you did to him the other night in the Long Branch."

"He never even saw me do that."

"Then why are you carrying a hidden gun, Bert?" Hank asked softly.

Bert Quinn stepped quickly back, frowning, under the shade of a wooden *ramada* that extended from the front of a corner feed store. He narrowed his eyes. "I

think I remember you now," he said. "You were in the
Bella Union the night I buffaloed the men in a brawl
and laid Barney Grant out cold."

Hank nodded. "You can go back further than that,
Bert Quinn. Think back. 'Way back. *Ten years back . . .*"

"Jesus," said Bert quietly. "It's impossible."

Hank shook his head. "It was ten years ago, Quinn."
Slowly Hank raised his left hand and touched the side of
his head. "You almost caved in my skull that night. You
had me sent to the pen on a rigged charge to cover up
some of Grant's rustling activities. You didn't give a good
goddamn that I was innocent. You hardly knew who I
was. Didn't it matter to you then? Didn't it matter to you
in those ten long years? No! I was forgotten as far as
you and Ned Grant were concerned."

Quinn held out a hand, palm upward, as though sup-
plicating this man whom he had wronged so long ago.
"I'll make amends, Hank. I've changed my life. Let me
make it up to you. I swear to God I will."

Hank shook his head.

"What's that?" asked Bert. He looked beyond Hank.

"No," said Hank quietly. "That old dodge won't work,
Bert. But I'm not a murderer. You're armed. Let's do
it the old-fashioned way. I often wanted to see how good
you really were shooting a pistol instead of smashing in
skulls with it."

"There's something going on over there," said Bert.
"I just saw a man leading a bunch of horses into that
alleyway."

Hank shook his head. He backed out of the shadow of
the *ramada* into the still brightly moonlit street. "When-
ever you're ready, Quinn," he challenged.

"For God's sake! Look out!" shouted Bert. He went
for his gun. Hank jumped to one side and made a fast
draw, crouching and then thrusting forward his Colt in
a line with his eyesight to fire from hip level. But Bert

Quinn had dropped before the bullet passed where he had been standing. He fired past Hank at Ken Dart who had raised his rifle to shoot at Hank. Ken Dart got the 200 grain .44/40 flatnosed slug right in the guts. He pitched forward into the street dropping his Winchester and clasping his belly. Bert's second slug hit him in the top of the head and killed him.

A rifleman came running toward the sound of the shooting. He threw up his rifle to aim at Bert but Hank Johnson fired through the drifting gunsmoke and the bullet struck Jim Downer in the right arm and spun him around. Hank's second bullet caught Downer low in the back and he pitched forward to lie still on the moonlit dust. "I know that man!" called out Bert. "He's one of Grant's *corrida!*"

Bert jumped sideways and looked up the alleyway toward the rear of the marshal's office just in time to see a man entering the rear door. Bert ran forward yelling back over his shoulder: "It's a jailbreak, Hank! I think that man we just saw was Ned Grant! They're likely after Barney! Cut around to the front!"

Bert ran toward the rear of the office.

Ned Grant came through the rear door of the office as Carl Barnett opened it for him. "There's someone on to what we're doing!" yelled Ned. "Get out into the alleyway and stop him!" Cal hurriedly brushed past Ned and ran into the alleyway.

Hank Johnson rounded the corner of the main street intersection. A tall, lean man stepped out of the doorway of the marshal's office and raised to fire at Hank. Hank dropped to his belly, thrust forward his Colt and fired three times at Jack Harding, who spun about and did an eerie dance of death as he staggered wide-eyed out into the middle of the street and fell onto the boardwalk on the far side of the street.

Hank jumped into a doorway and flipped open the

loading gate of his Colt to eject the empty hulls and to cram fresh cartridges into the chambers.

Carl Barnett raised his Colt as he saw Bert Quinn jump behind a shed down the alleyway. Cal Betz came running up behind him. Carl whirled and fired from the hip dropping Cal Betz flat on his back with a bullet in his left thigh. "You crazy sonofabitch!" yelled Cal. "Look out behind you!" Carl whirled in time to see Bert Quinn snapshoot at him. Carl fired and then ducked back into the rear doorway of the office.

Ned turned the key in the lock of the cell door. "Come on, son," he said. "Your old man's come to get you."

Barney blanched. "I ain't going out there," he said. "I'm liable to get killed."

"You'll get killed if you stay here!" yelled Ned. He thrust a Colt into Barney's hand. "Come on! We've got to make a break for it!" Ned shoved Barney toward the rear door of the office. "Lead the way, Carl!" yelled Ned.

"Go to hell!" snapped Carl Barnett. "You do your own killing from now on!" He brushed past Barney and Ned and jumped over Newly, buffaloed unconscious and tied up, who was lying on the floor of the office. He burst through the front doorway and turned to run toward the alleyway and the horses.

"Stand where you are!" warned Hank Johnson from a doorway across the street.

Carl whirled and fired from the hip. The bullet slapped through a store window behind Hank. Hank had jumped to one side. He fired from the hip and the bullet fanned past Carl's head. Carl ran for the corner and then turned to fire as Hank ran toward him. Hank's bullet caught him low in the guts and as he pitched forward another bullet hit him in the heart. He was dead when he hit the street.

Hank quickly reloaded and ducked into a doorway next to the front of the marshal's office.

Barney Grant ran out into the street. His eyes were

wild. He saw the sprawled bodies of Jack Harding and Carl Burnett lying in the street. Men, awakened by the intense shooting, were shouting to each other. Gunsmoke still drifted in the windless air.

"Stand where you are!" yelled Hank Johnson.

Barney ran awkwardly toward the alleyway, presenting his back to Hank Johnson. Hank raised his Colt and then lowered it. He could not shoot a man in the back even if it was Barney Grant. Hank turned as Ned Grant came charging through the front doorway of the marshal's office. Ned threw a snap-shot at Hank and ducked back into the office. He slammed shut the door and threw the bolt.

Hank raced after the panicky, fleeing man. He rounded the alleyway corner. Barney ran through the side alleyway toward Mark Manton who was holding the horses, now skittered by the shooting.

Hank reached the intersection of the alleyway that ran behind the marshal's office. A man was dragging himself along by his hands and elbows with sweat streaming down his face. His left leg dragged awkwardly behind him. "Don't shoot, for Christ's sake!" yelled Cal Betz to Hank Johnson. Hank made the mistake of looking after the fleeing Barney. Cal still held his Colt in his right hand. He fired at Hank. The slug hit Hank in the right shoulder and spun him about. He dropped his pistol from a nerveless hand and crashed backward against a shed wall and then sank down to the ground. Cal raised his pistol to finish off Hank.

Bert Quinn saw Cal wound Hank and drop him to the ground. Bert ran toward Cal, passing the rear of the marshal's office. A pistol cracked hollowly within the rear doorway of the office. Bert staggered as the bullet hit him low in the left side but he managed to fire and hit Cal Betz in the rear of the skull. Bert staggered sideways, dropping his smoking Colt. He crashed against the rear of a shed.

Ned Grant came quickly out of the rear doorway with his pistol pointed at Bert Quinn and an unholy grin on his hard face. "Quinn!" he said. He thrust the pistol forward and cocked the spur hammer. The Colt blasted flame and smoke.

Bert Quinn's body jerked as a second slug hit him in the right shoulder. He thrust his left hand into his coat pocket for his Derringer with the last reserve he had of strength and will.

"Grant!" yelled Hank.

Ned Grant made the fatal mistake of turning to look at Hank. Ned Grant's body jerked twice as two soft 41-caliber slugs hit him over the heart and he fell forward to die in the muck of the alleyway. Bert Quinn dropped the smoking Derringer and sank down to the ground. He looked through the drifting gunsmoke to see Hank Johnson holding his right shoulder and walking slowly toward him.

Barney Grant came up behind Mark Manton. "Let's get the hell out of here!" he yelled. "They're killing them all!"

"Where's your old man!" yelled Mark as he mounted his horse.

"Who the hell cares!" yelled Barney. He looked after the rest of the horses who were now stampeding through the dying moonlight. "Give me that horse!" he yelled at Mark.

Mark turned the horse on the forehand and bent low as he struck the steel into the flanks of the horse. Barney's bullet caught him just over the kidneys. He fell sideways from the saddle with his right foot caught in the stirrup and the horse galloped off dragging Mark down the hard rutted street bouncing about like a rag doll. He was dead within two blocks.

Barney turned slowly. Half a dozen armed citizens of Dodge were running toward him. Barney dropped his Colt and slowly raised his right arm. "I don't want to die," he pleaded fearfully.

"You won't *tonight,* mister," said the first of the men. "When you do will be up to the judge at your trial."

Hank Johnson had knelt beside Bert Quinn. Bert was looking toward the waning moon. "It was a damned good fight, wasn't it, Hank?" he quietly asked. He looked at Hank. "Are you all right?"

Hank nodded. "You'll be all right, too," he promised.

Bert shook his head. "I've always heard it said you'll know when your time is up." He nodded. "That's right. I know now . . ."

Men gathered along the alleyway, quietly talking, looking at the sprawled bodies of the dead and at the two friends—Bert Quinn and Hank Johnson.

Doc Adams came hurriedly into the alleyway. He knelt beside Bert Quinn, opening his coat, vest and shirt to examine the two wounds. He looked at Bert's calm, peaceful looking face. "I know," said Bert quietly.

"Let me look at that shoulder of yours, Hank," said Doc.

Hank held up a hand. "Wait," he said.

Doc stepped back.

Hank cradled Bert's head and shoulders on his lap. He bent his head. In a little while Bert's body moved and then stiffened.

Doc walked away from the two friends.

The gunsmoke had drifted off. The moon was dying. Dodge City was very quiet again. Somewhere in the distance a dog howled.